THE ROCKER
WHO *Cherishes*
Me

USA TODAY & WSJ BESTSELLING AUTHOR

TERRI ANNE
BROWNING

DEDICATION

To the man who cherishes me like no else ever has or ever will. I love you.

Then. Now. Forever.

There are people in everyone's lives that you couldn't live without. I am lucky enough to have friends and loved ones that are my rock, my shoulder to cry on, or bitch to, or any number of crazy things. Without them I would truly be lost. They talk me down from imaginary ledges that I want to jump off of when my characters won't go where I want them to.

The biggest thank you is for YOU, my amazing fans. You have helped me reach a dream I never thought would be possible. I could never show you enough how much you are loved and appreciated by me.

Love TAB

PROLOGUE

MARISSA

Nine Years Ago

With a moan, I turned my head away from the television. A sob was already trapped in my throat even before the vomit made its way into my mouth. I wretched until I was dry heaving then rested my head on the hospital bed while Mary Beth rubbed my back soothingly with one hand and held a cool washcloth to my face with the other. Moaning, I just lay there, wishing the nausea away.

I'd had a chemo treatment that morning—my second this week—and these violent bouts of vomiting were a bonus to all that chemical fun. While other teenage girls my age were worried about blemishes, finding a date for the homecoming dance, or even if she was going to pass her calculus final, I had other things on my mind. Like staying strong just a little longer until a bone morrow donor was found.

Fortunately, a matching donor had finally been found. It had only taken a little over a year to find one, and only then because my brother and his band had made a public appeal because time was quickly running out...

The chemo I'd had today was only a taste of what I would be getting in the morning before the doctors took bone marrow from my donor and put it into me. And after that it was a wait and see game. Wait to see if the transplant would help... Or if I would die, because this was the last option.

Over the last two years I'd gone through all the stages that a person of any age would go through when the doctors informed them that they had an aggressive form of cancer. Denial, anger, grief. You name it, I've felt it. But in the last few months, I had finally accepted that this illness might kill me.

I was sixteen years old. My life might not have always been perfect, but I've always felt loved. I've always had what I needed, and in the last few years I've been given everything I've ever wanted. So, if I did die I was going to go knowing that my life had been a good one.

There was just one thing I desperately wanted while I could still ask for it. And tonight, before I was transferred from this hospital room that had been my home for the last six weeks into an isolated room where only the nurses and doctors would be able to enter, I was going to ask. Beg if I had to.

With that thought firmly in mind I raised my head and took the washcloth from my adopted mother. Mary Beth took me in when my father died. She and her husband could have let me go into foster care, but when they gained custody of my brother—their nephew—ten years ago, they had asked for me too. Since I'd had no other family except for Liam, it was either go with them or into the system. Mary Beth, having always wanted a daughter but unable to have more children after the birth of her only son, had spoiled me rotten from that day on.

"Here, baby. Rinse out your mouth." Mary Beth offered me a cup of water and I took it gratefully. Swishing some water around in my mouth I spit it out in the bucket beside my bed then did the same to the mouthwash she handed over.

"When will they get here?" I whispered because my throat was aching from all the vomiting I'd done over the last few hours.

Mary Beth glanced down at her watch then over at the door. "They called from Chattanooga. So they should be here anytime now, baby."

I bit my lip and glanced at the clock. It was nearly nine at night. If my brother and his bandmates didn't get here soon then I wasn't going to get to see them tonight and I knew that I wouldn't get to see them in the morning. Which meant that I would only get to see anyone through a window for the next few weeks. No human contact. Anxiety over not getting to see my brother—and other people—made my stomach turn over and tears stung my eyes.

With most of her face covered with a mask to keep from breathing her germs on me, Mary Beth leaned forward and pressed a kiss to my temple through the paper barrier. "They will get here, Marissa. I promise."

I couldn't speak through the knot of tears in my throat so I nodded and kept my eyes on the clock. Liam and the band had been touring for the last two months. Tabloids have been giving him and his band, OtherWorld, grief for not being with me while I was so sick, and I knew that it was killing him not to be here with me. I wanted him here so badly that my heart couldn't help but cry. But I also knew that OtherWorld and touring was his job and without that job my treatment wouldn't have been what it was. There would have been no money for the team of specialists that had been taking care of me day and night. No money for the crazy expensive chemo treatments or the pain and nausea medication.

The tour had ended last night, and OtherWorld's tour bus had been driving since the last concert ended to get them here.

"How about a movie?" Mary Beth offered as she lifted the DVD box that held my favorite movie, *The Wizard of Oz*. Bless Mary Beth, because she had sat and watched that movie with me a million times since I'd been diagnosed with leukemia two years ago.

I forced a smile and nodded as she placed the movie into the DVD player that Liam had had delivered the day after he found out I had been admitted into the hospital. Along with the DVD player had been a stack of my favorite movies, including *The Wizard of Oz* and a few other Judy Garland movies, and a huge teddy bear. The teddy bear hadn't been from Liam, and even though I'd given up sleeping with stuffed animals years ago, I'd slept with that bear every night until my first chemo treatment and Mary Beth had to take the bear home.

The house had just fallen on the witch when my hospital room door opened with a suddenness that made me jump. Raising my head, I found four men in masks, scrubs, and booties over their shoes. I sat up and a grin broke across my face for the first time in what felt like forever. I took the four of them in, recognizing them all even though most of their faces were covered.

Axton was the first one. He was leaner than the rest, but he was taller than two of the four. His hazel eyes crinkled at the corners, but I could see the concern in their depths. That concern was mirrored in the other three men's eyes. Behind him stood Zander, whom I recognized because his hands were inked up just as much as the rest of his body. The word OTHER was across the knuckles of his right hand while the word WORLD was across the knuckles of his left. As always, Devlin was right beside his best friend. Dev was the second tallest of the band, but even if he weren't I would still know it was him from his dark tan, those unique aquamarine eyes, and his long nearly black hair pulled into a ponytail and stuffed under a surgical cap.

The man behind the first three pushed forward and Mary Beth stood to let him take her place on the edge of my bed. Liam's arms wrapped around me carefully, as if he was afraid to break me. I swallowed another lump of tears and closed my eyes to keep them from spilling down my face as my brother held me close.

"You made it," I finally whispered after he'd been holding me for a few minutes.

"Of course I did. Did you think I would miss getting to hold you one more time?" He pressed a kiss to the top of my head through his surgical mask. "Everything's going to be okay now, Rissa. You'll be okay."

I nodded, not wanting him to know how unsure I was of that. I was so sick. So weak. So. Tired. I didn't want my brother to know how close to just giving up I was. He had too many demons to fight as it was. I couldn't let him know that it was a battle to keep going.

As Liam moved so that his bandmates could hug me, I finally let myself think about the one member who was missing. My heart had sunk a little the moment I'd realized he wasn't here with the rest of them. Where was he? Had he not wanted to see me? Didn't he care? I felt horrible because he had been the only one I'd really wanted to see, but I tried to keep a smile on my face as Zander, Devlin, and Axton did their best to make me laugh.

"Okay," Axton said as he hugged me again. "We're going to go so that Wroth can come in. He needed a few minutes to himself."

My eyes widened at Axton's confession, but my heart flew skyward as I realized that Wroth was actually there. He was there! I couldn't help that my smile was even brighter as I let the three huge rockers hug and kiss me. *Wroth is here. I am going to get to see him after all.*

Liam stood as well. "I don't want to go, but I know he's gonna want to see you alone. So I'm going to go crash in the waiting room. If you need anything let me know, okay Rissa? Anything and it's yours."

I rolled my eyes at him. From that very first enormous paycheck he'd gotten with OtherWorld he'd done nothing but spoil me. "I know, Liam. But all I really want is right here." I hugged him hard one last time and he took Mary Beth's hand and they left me alone. Anxiously waiting for the only person I felt like I would die if I didn't see.

A few minutes passed. I bit my dry lip, trying not to feel hurt that Wroth hadn't rushed in here to see me as soon as humanly possible. If it had been the other way around, I wouldn't have been able to keep away even for a second. It might sound like I had a silly schoolgirl crush on Wroth Niall but that wasn't the case.

I loved him. Plain and simple. There have been times I wished that I didn't love him, but honestly I couldn't have fallen for a better guy. Wroth knows what's important in life. He's served his country as a marine, used his enlistment bonus to pull the farm that has been in his family for five generations out of financial trouble, and treats me and his momma like we are fine china.

When the door to my room opened again, I held my breath until six foot five inches of solid muscle walked in. At the first sight of him all the tears that I'd been able to hold back for Mary Beth and Liam and the others came flooding to the surface and a sob escaped me before I could call it back. Brown eyes darkened, that strong jaw covered in a surgical mask flexed with emotion and I held my arms out like I was a little kid.

A groan that sounded more like a growl was torn from him and he crossed to my bed in just a few strides before dropping down next to me on the mattress. Strong arms wrapped around me tightly but still with tenderness, his hands wrapping around thin dark hair and pulling my head against his strong chest. Neither of us spoke as he held me and I silently cried. In that moment I knew that I didn't want to die, even if I had assured myself I was okay with death. I didn't want to leave this man behind. I wanted more moments with his arms around me, more moments just being beside him.

We sat like that for a long while, but it didn't feel like long enough. Wroth pulled back, wiping big fat teardrops from my cheeks with his thumbs. "How are you feeling?" he asked in a huskier than normal voice. I loved the sound of Wroth's voice. Some people said it was scary, almost terrifying at times depending on his mood, but I'd always been drawn to it. I loved that gravely, smoky sound.

"I'm better now," I promised him. At least emotionally better now that he was there. I was still nauseous though, and it was a feat in and of itself to keep from vomiting in front of him despite the fact that there was nothing in me to throw up.

"You've lost more weight since I last saw you." His eyes narrowed as he brushed his hands over my hair. "And your hair is dry and thin…"

I felt my cheeks fill with pink and I pulled back from him a little, hating that I was already looking like the sick person I was. "The chemo is already working its magic. By the end of everything I will be bald. I probably won't even have eyelashes."

"You'll still be just as beautiful without all that hair, Mari."

Pleasure made my heart leap. I loved it when he called me Mari. He was the only one to call me that, and only rarely, but when he did I felt like I could fly to the moon and back. Leaning forward again, I laid my head on his chest once more, soothed by the steady beat of his heart. Wroth held me like that for a little while, but then moved us so that he was practically lying beside me with my head pillowed on his chest. With a content sigh, I wrapped an arm over his hard stomach and closed my eyes. I could sleep like this forever.

Of course the night nurse wasn't going to let that happen. With a tap on the door it opened and there stood my warden. She gave a disapproving frown at the sight of Wroth lying on the bed with me. "Visiting hours will be over in five minutes. Your friend needs to be going soon."

Wroth started to move but I shook my head as I sat up. "You said it won't be over for five more minutes. He can stay until then." When the nurse started to protest I glared at her. "Five more minutes!"

Shaking her head the nurse backed out of the room and let the door close behind her. Wroth sat up beside me, his arms going around me once again. "I'd better go, Mari. You need to rest for tomorrow."

"But I rest better when you're with me," I grumbled.

I could tell he was smiling by the way his eyes crinkled a little at the corners. Wroth rarely smiled so there weren't any lines around his eyes yet. "We'll do this again one day. When you're all better."

I couldn't help but pout. Couldn't the doctors sterilize Wroth and let him stay with me for the duration?

"Promise?" Fresh tears suddenly blurred my vision and made my throat ache.

"I swear," he said and then hugged me tightly for another moment before starting to stand.

My chance to ask for the one thing I wanted the most, the one thing that would give me a reason to keep fighting until I couldn't fight any more, was quickly slipping away. Gathering my courage, I just blurted it out. "Will you kiss me, Wroth?"

His big body paused halfway up and he dropped back down next to me. Even though I couldn't see the rest of his face, his eyes told me that he was shocked by my question. Wroth hugged me all the time, but he'd never given me so much as a peck on the cheek. I couldn't remember him even ever kissing his mother. So I knew that my question, my plea for a kiss, had stunned him.

He didn't answer right away. I could see his mind working, wondering what I was thinking even asking him such a thing. Some people might think I was crossing a line, but despite his relationship with my brother I wasn't related to Wroth in any way. His mother and Liam's mother had been sisters. My mother… Well I had no idea who or even where she was. She ran off just a few months after I was born, unable to handle a baby let alone one on top of a stepson.

"Mari…"

He was using the nickname I loved so much, but I could tell he was about to let me down easy. I couldn't let him. I needed his kiss to get me through the weeks that were about to follow. "Please, Wroth. I'll never ask you for anything ever again. I promise. Just… Please. One kiss. I…" I hated thinking the next words, let alone saying them but I was desperate. "I might not…" My voice broke, and I was unable to finish the sentence, but I saw the way the skin around his eyes tightened. "…I want to know what a real kiss feels like."

"You really know how to gut a guy, huh?" He shook his head, but didn't try to stand again.

I didn't answer, because I didn't know how to respond. Was he really gutted at the thought of losing me? When I just sat there, staring up at him, my plea still in my eyes, he groaned. "Mari, you know I'd give you anything you want." With a curse under his breath, he raised his hands and cupped both sides of my face. "You're so beautiful, girl."

The way he said that one word made something deep inside of me melt. 'Girl' had come out more like a growl than an actual word. I shivered as he lowered his head until his nose skimmed mine through his mask. Reaching up I pulled the mask down until his lips were free. My eyes, hungry for the sight of the rest of his face, drank in the sight of dark stubble shadowing his jaw, that strong nose, and damp full lips. His face wasn't traditionally handsome, it was too strong and square. But his ruggedness, the badass air he put off attached to all that strength made him sexy in a way that women melted over. I'd never been immune to him, doubted I ever would be.

When those warm, full lips brushed over mine my heart stopped. It was an innocent kiss, there was no passion in it, but this wasn't about passion. It was about having something to hold onto, a memory I could fall back on when I wanted to give up.

He was actually giving me the kiss I asked for and it was so perfect, so incredibly amazing. My first kiss was so sweet it brought tears to my eyes. They spilled free and when Wroth tasted them he quickly raised his head. "Mari?"

"Th-thank you, Wroth," I whispered. "That was perfect."

Still cupping my face he offered me a small smile that didn't reach his eyes. "Anything for you, sweetheart."

The door opened again and there stood my nurse, tapping her foot. I shot her another glare, but Wroth sighed and pressed a kiss to my forehead before standing. "I'll be in the waiting room, sweetheart."

"I don't want you to go."

"I'm not going anywhere. As long as you're here, I'll be here too." He winked down at me. "Goodnight, Mari."

I swallowed hard, trying not to cry again until he was out the door. "Goodnight, Wroth."

CHAPTER 1

MARISSA

Present Day

The smell of coffee pulled me out of a dream-filled sleep. I blinked open my eyes, trying to fight the melancholy that washed over me as I tried to pull the dream back, attempting to remember why I was feeling so sad all of a sudden. I knew that it had to have been a dream about Wroth, because he was all I seemed to be able to dream about these days. And I knew that it hadn't been one of the many wet dreams I'd been having since I could freaking have wet dreams, but had intensified since the spring tour over a year ago. I also knew that it wasn't even the dream where I kicked his ass, because those dreams always left me feeling pissed off but a little vindicated when I woke up.

Fighting the urge to cry, and angry because I didn't know why but did know the most likely cause, I crawled out of bed and pulled a thin robe over my tank top and shorts pajamas. My long hair was a tangled mess so I pulled the thick tresses into a knot on top of my head and slowly made my way down the hall. The television was on in the living room to some show on *E!* but I refrained from rolling my eyes at my roommate's reality show addiction.

The scent of coffee was getting stronger and my own addiction was calling my name. I was a coffee addict, and since moving to New York last year, that addiction had only grown since there was a different coffee shop on every corner. As I entered the kitchen I had eyes only for the coffee pot, so when the refrigerator door closed with a thump, I turned my head to glance at Linc.

Only to wish I hadn't when my gaze landed on his very naked body. Well, damn! It wasn't the first time I'd seen Linc Spencer's dick in the last twelve months. It wasn't even the fifth time. And like every time before, and every female with red blood running through her veins, my gaze lingered on his very impressive man parts. Sadly, however, I felt nothing below the neck at the sight of such male perfection. Which was probably a good thing, seeing as that lusting after my very gay roommate would only lead to hurt feelings because he would never be able to feel that way about me.

"Morning, Rissa," Linc greeted me with a smirk because he knew exactly what I was gaping at.

Pink filling my already warm cheeks, I turned back to the coffee pot and poured myself a gigantic mug full of the strong brew. Thankfully

Jesse Thornton had given Linc the recipe for his special morning coffee during OtherWorld's and Demon's Wing's fall tour and Linc had started making it when he and Natalie had returned back in November. My other roommate wouldn't go near the coffee pot now, but Linc and I seemed to be attached to it in the mornings.

"Morning," I murmured before taking my first sip of rich coffee.

"Tonight's the night," he informed me as he set a dozen eggs, a whole tomato, onion, mushrooms and spinach on the counter by the stove where a pan was already sprayed and waiting for him to make a mammoth omelet. "Are you ready?"

Instead of answering him, I took a bigger gulp of coffee to give myself a moment to decide if I was ready for tonight or not. Last week my brother had asked me to have dinner with everyone tonight. Everyone being all the members of OtherWorld, the members of Demon's Wings and their families, and the two new bands that would be touring with them over the summer. A tour that would start in three days. A tour that I didn't want to go on, but foresaw my brother asking me to join him on anyway.

Liam had begged and pleaded for me to join him on the fall tour, not wanting me to be alone in New York for two months since both my roommates would be gone. But I hadn't been able to face another tour. Not when the wounds of the last tour had been so fresh. This tour was going to be considerably longer than the fall tour.

Fourteen weeks long actually, so I knew that Liam wasn't going to deal well with me staying in New York alone for that long.

I didn't want to worry my brother. He was doing so great with his recovery not only from the accident that had nearly killed him last year, but also with his drug addiction. He had been clean for nineteen months now, the longest he has ever been clean since he had started using when he was in his teens. But I always worried that he would eventually fall back into old habits, was terrified that he would turn to the drugs if I stressed him out. After watching his struggle with heroin back when I had been so sick with cancer, I couldn't help but worry that I was one of the reasons he had needed the drugs in the first place.

Still, I didn't want to go on a stupid tour with stupid rockers... Grimacing, I shook my head. Okay, so only one of them was stupid. So stupid that I wanted to kick him in the head a few times in the hopes of fixing his stupid problem.

I was definitely conflicted about tonight. Unsure if I could say no to my brother, but knowing that I needed to. I couldn't handle being that close to Wroth Niall again. I'd moved from Tennessee to New York City to get away from him. Made sure I was busy when he was in town, and had even gone so far as staying in a hotel when he'd camped out in the apartment for an entire weekend waiting for me to come home. The closest I've been to him was on Valentine's Day for Austin Bradshaw's wedding and then the after party which had taken place in a maternity ward waiting room where the reception had ended up being because Dallas had gone into labor.

Even then I had avoided him, going as far as boxing myself into a corner with some of Dallas's family members. It wouldn't be any different tonight. I didn't want to be near Wroth. I didn't want to see his handsome face, or smell his spicy scent. I didn't want to look at him and worry if he'd been getting enough sleep, been eating enough, or was dealing with his demons— all the things I'd made sure of and worried about when I'd lived in the same house with him.

"I'm sure it will be fun," I finally told him with a smile that hurt my cheeks because it was so forced.

Linc raised a brow at me, letting me know that he didn't believe me, but didn't call me on it. Instead he started putting together two omelets. I topped off my coffee and took my seat at the kitchen table. When Linc put my omelet in front of me I nodded my thanks and devoured the deliciousness. Linc went to put some clothes on and by the time he returned, I was half finished. When my plate was empty, I sat back to finish my coffee and waited for Natalie to join us.

Natalie wasn't working this morning, but I knew she would have things to do before tonight's dinner. As Emmie Armstrong's right hand, Natalie worked her ass off. Emmie demanded a hundred and ten percent effort from all her employees and Nat gave her a hundred and fifty, going above and beyond for her boss.

When the beautiful girl walked into the kitchen, she was dressed for the day, but her face was clenched and I knew it was because she was just as reluctant to see certain rockers as I was. Unfortunately for her, she had to deal with those rockers on a regular basis. She didn't have the luxury of ignoring them because she worked for them—him.

Moving to the fridge, Natalie pulled out a cup of Greek yogurt and a bottle of water. Standing by the sink, she ate her small breakfast in silence. The way her eyes stared into nothingness I knew she was in a world of her own so I let her stay there, sipping at my coffee while Linc finished up his breakfast.

Linc took both our plates to the sink and rinsed them off. Dropping a kiss on top of Natalie's head before grabbing a bottle of water from the fridge, he gave me a small, tight smile. "Well, I gotta go wake your brother up. His lazy ass has had long enough to sleep in."

A glance at the clock on the microwave showed that it was just now after seven. I grinned, because until his accident and Linc had taken over as his PT and then his personal trainer, Liam had slept until two in the afternoon every day. Since Linc had been helping him get into shape, Liam's whole personality had changed. He wasn't as moody, wasn't as scary quiet, and was a lot more outgoing. He also had about thirty pounds of muscle on him, when before he'd been practically skin and bones. It had done nothing but make skank groupies drool over him all the more. Yuck!

"Have fun," I told Linc.

Linc's eyes turned mischievous. Linc was into pretty boys, and they didn't get more pretty boy looking than my brother with the exception of the Stevenson brothers. Liam had a face that, despite all his years of heavy drug use, was still young looking. I knew that Linc would never put the moves on Liam, but I was sure that he was more than happy to scream and yell at my brother every morning when he worked out with him. "I will, but he probably won't."

Laughing, I stood to refill my mug and watched as he left the kitchen. At the sound of the front door shutting behind him, I finally turned to Natalie, figuring she'd had enough time stewing over whatever was going through her head. "What are you doing this morning?"

"Shaving my head," she informed me matter-of-factly before tossing the now empty cup of yogurt in the trashcan.

"What?" I was sure that I had heard her wrong. Natalie had hair that was past her shoulders. It was thick, glossy and freaking perfect in my opinion. It only added to her beauty and I would consider it a travesty to shave all of that glorious hair off.

Natalie shrugged, but didn't elaborate. Grimacing, I sat back down at the table, figuring that her wanting to shave her head was to spite someone. Devlin Cutter, most likely. "Okay, then I'll come with you. I need to get a trim." I hadn't cut my hair since it had finally grown back after my battle with leukemia, only trimming the ends off every few months to keep it healthy. My hair was past my waist now and I would probably cry if I ever even thought about shaving it all off. I've been bald before, I wasn't ever going there again, let alone on purpose. "What else are you doing today?"

She gulped down half the bottle of water before hugging me from behind. "So many things, that I want to hide in a hole and hope that Emmie never finds me. Want to come with me? I could use the company instead of having to listen to my own thoughts for the rest of the day."

"Sounds good to me. And then we'll go shopping for a killer dress to make douchebag idiots regret every stupid decision they've ever made." I didn't shop often, but when I did it was with a purpose in mind. Today's purpose? Make Wroth Niall sorry he ever broke my heart.

"Damn straight." Smacking a kiss to my cheek, Natalie pulled away. "Thanks, Rissa."

I frowned. "What for?"

"For understanding. It sucks balls, but I'm kind of glad we're both in the same boat." She tossed her now empty water bottle in the trash. "I fucking hate guys."

"Me too, sweetie. Me too."

CHAPTER 2

WROTH

The club was dead when the cab I'd taken from the hotel pulled up in front of it. Dead in the sense that there was only one bouncer standing in front of a velvet rope with about ten girls and five guys standing behind it. I was early, hoping to catch Marissa before everyone else arrived. Once the place filled up with our friends and the rest of the bands that were touring with us this summer, I knew that I wouldn't have a chance of speaking to her privately all night.

I'd been trying for months now to get her to just speak to me. She wasn't having any of it though. Somehow she seemed to always know when I was in the city and made herself scarce. I'd even been desperate enough to camp out on her roommate's couch in their living room for three solid days in hopes of getting five minutes to talk to her. She hadn't come home and finally Linc had told me that Marissa wasn't going to come home until she knew for sure that I was gone.

I hadn't wanted to be the reason Marissa wasn't sleeping in her own bed, hated the thought of whose bed she might have been in during that time. So I'd left and then gone back to Tennessee the next day when Liam had come to my hotel room to tell me to leave his sister alone.

"She doesn't want anything to do with you, Wroth." Liam had told me as he'd glared at me across the span of my hotel room. The closeness that my cousin and I had had in the past had been annihilated when I'd done something he'd thought was the worst crime on the planet. Broken his sister's heart. I could have told him that what he and his sister—and everyone else for that matter—thought had happened that crazy night hadn't been what they thought. I didn't because I knew that it would only be a waste of breath and I didn't owe anyone but Marissa an explanation. "Just go back to the farm and when she decides she wants to talk to you, I'll let you know. Until then, stay the fuck away from her."

I'd gone home, reluctantly, but only because I believed what Liam had said was the truth. Marissa just wasn't ready to talk to me. She wasn't ready to hear my side of what had happened that fucked up night. So I would respect her wishes until she was ready.

But that had been months ago and I was losing my fucking mind without her. I couldn't sleep, only ate because my housekeeper had threatened to quit when I'd wasted the food she would place in front of me. I'd always hated that fucking old hag, but she'd always been nice to Marissa and so I would continue to keep her around because I held out hope that my girl would one day come back home.

When the fans standing behind the velvet rope saw me, the chicks started screaming and a few of them even dared to raise their shirts and flash me their tits. I glared disinterestedly in their direction for a half second before rolling my eyes and stepping past the bouncer and into the club. There were only a few other people inside. Emmie and Nik with their nanny, Felicity, along with their two kids Mia and Jagger. Lucy, Harris, and Devlin were helping set up some of the food that a caterer was putting out on the bar top. Other than that the place was quiet since there wasn't any music playing yet.

"Wroth," Nik called from across the club. He was grinning and holding up a glass of what looked like tea. I grimaced, figuring that was going to be the hardest drink on the menu tonight.

At the sound of my name, Devlin turned from setting another large pan on the bar top. He nodded his head in greeting and I tipped mine back. I'd seen him last night when I'd been checking into the same hotel we were staying in for the next few days. Unlike Dev, who always seemed to want the penthouse suite, I didn't need anything other than a bed and a bathroom and was staying in one of the hotel's blandest rooms several floors down.

It wasn't that I didn't have the money to afford the penthouse; no, if anything I earned more money than any of the other members of OtherWorld with the exception of Axton who got paid out the ass for the reality show *America's Rocker*. The money I made from my farm was enough to let me live an above comfortable life without the need to even touch the money I made from OtherWorld. I just couldn't stand over-the-top things.

As soon as I reached Nik he handed over a glass of iced tea and I took it with a nod in thanks. "How you been?" I asked.

"Crazy busy, but nothing new about that." Nik pointed his thumb over his shoulder where his wife was talking to some chick in a waitress's outfit and a sheet of paper in her hand. "I don't know how she does what she does without losing her mind. I've been helping her for the last few days get everything ready for the tour and I've been about to pull my hair out with just the simple tasks she's given me."

I nodded. "Emmie is a superhero, man."

"Momma's a superhero?" a little voice suddenly demanded and I looked down to find Mia standing just behind me, her big green eyes so much like her mother's, huge with surprise and awe. "For real, Daddy?"

Nik laughed. "Yeah, I guess she is, baby doll."

"Awesome. Can I have some cake now, Daddy?"

That she accepted her father's word so easily made me smile while my friend told his daughter that she had to eat something a little more filling than cake before she got her dessert. With an exasperated sigh as if her world had to be put on pause for the moment until she could get her cake, Mia walked off to ask her nanny for a plate of 'real food'.

Seeing Mia reminded me of the little girl that Marissa had been when she'd come to live with me and my parents. She'd only been six, a little older than Mia was now. She'd been so lost after the death of her father, so afraid of someone else leaving her because she only had Liam left. It had taken years for her to fully trust that my parents loved her just as much as they loved me and Liam because she wasn't related to them by blood.

Just before Marissa had been diagnosed with cancer, my father had died of a heart attack and she had been devastated, but nowhere close to how she'd been when my mother had passed away. Marissa had still been in isolation when my mother had had her heart attack and died only hours later. The look on her face as I'd watched the doctors deliver the news while I'd watched through the window that was my only connection to her at the time had nearly brought me to my knees.

That same look of loss had still been in her eyes every time we would go visit my mother's grave. And it was there, standing over the flower covered grave of Mary Beth Niall with our shared pain over the loss of such an amazing woman, that I had realized how I really felt for Marissa…

"It's been three years and I still miss her," Marissa murmured as she bent to replace the bouquet of dried roses with a fresh one. Yellow roses had been my mother's favorite flower and Marissa made sure she had fresh ones every month.

I clenched my jaw, nodding my agreement. When my mother had died three years ago I'd been too busy worrying about Marissa and her recovery to really deal with my own sense of loss over my mother's sudden death. I hadn't even cried at her funeral because I'd been so worried about the distraught sixteen-year-old waiting for me to get back to stand outside her hospital room. By the time Marissa had been recovering from her illness and then considered in remission, Mom had been gone for nearly six months.

The first day home, Marissa had demanded I take her to see Mom grave, which was right beside of my father's. From then on we would visit together at least once a month, and if I was off on tour with OtherWorld she always visited by herself with my foreman watching over her.

Straightening, Marissa turned to wrap her arms around my waist. Tears glinted in her blue eyes as she gazed up at me. "She loved you so much, you know. You could do nothing wrong in her eyes." She laughed sadly, shaking her head, causing her shoulder length hair to fall forward. "You're a good man, Wroth."

A few strands of hair stuck to her tear dampened cheek and I lifted a hand to brush them away. But the feel of her skin under my fingertips was so soft that I couldn't help but let them linger as I skimmed my thumb over her cheek. I'd never known skin could be so silky soft. The feel of it made my body hardened and I released her, disgusted with myself for feeling desire for the girl in my arms.

Hastily I pulled away from her. "I'm not always a good man, Mari," I told her honestly. She didn't know how bad of a man I'd been when I was overseas in the marines. Killing people that could have been innocents for all I knew because I was ordered to, because it was kill or be killed. And I definitely wasn't a good man right now when the sudden need to kiss and touch and make bone melting hot love to her was overwhelming me.

I stared down at my mother's headstone for a moment, silently asking for her forgiveness for feeling this way for the one person I'd always promised her I would protect and cherish. The feeling of relief for her forgiveness didn't come and I turned away with the sudden choking feeling of being unable to breathe. "We need to go," I grumbled over my shoulder.

Marissa didn't protest as she climbed into my truck and I drove us back to the farm. She was quiet on the ride home, shooting me concerned glances across the seat. My fingers gripped the steering wheel so hard that my knuckles were turning white and aching as I attempted to control my sudden need to reach across the seat and pull her into my arms and devour those luscious lips she was now tormenting by biting them.

As soon as we got home, I locked myself in my room and took care of the ache that was tightening my balls. But no sooner than I'd taken care of it I heard her voice outside my door as she asked if I was okay and my body began to ache all over again. It would have been so easy to just open the door and pull her into my room. I could have spent hours teaching her all about the pleasures of sex. There wasn't anything wrong with it. She was nineteen, after all, more than old enough to have a lover.

My dick pulsed at pictures filling my mind at all the things I could teach Marissa. But it was my heart and brain that screamed at me that I wasn't going to do that. No way was I going to take something that I wasn't good enough for. Right then it was only desire fueling my need for her, not love. Although it would be all too easy to fall for her. But Marissa was too sweet, too pure and innocent to defile her just for the pleasure of having her tight little body wrapped around my dick.

I cared about Marissa, and I wanted her with a need that I'd never felt in my entire life, but I couldn't contaminate her with my dirty past. I wouldn't.

The feel of a soft, cool hand on my arm jerked me back from my memories of the first time I'd realized that I wanted Marissa. Startled, I looked up into a pair of blue eyes, but they weren't the blue ones that I had come to love. Dallas gave me a small smile as she took the empty glass of tea from my hands and replaced it with a fresh one. "Easy there, tiger. It's just me."

I blinked at her and then glanced around the room, noticing that more people had arrived but there was still no sign of the one person I ached to see with every fiber of my being. I glanced down at my watch and realized that it was more than thirty minutes past the time the dinner was supposed to start. "Where's Rissa?"

Dallas shrugged. "I have no idea. I guess she and Natalie are running late." She patted me on the arm. "Don't worry, big guy. She'll be here soon enough though."

CHAPTER 3

MARISSA

When the cab pulled to a stop in front of one of New York City's most exclusive clubs, I didn't blink. The fact that there was a line to get into the club that wrapped all the way around the block didn't surprise me either. What bothered me was that they were all lined up, despite the sign that was on the door that said that the club was closed for a private party tonight. Obviously everyone knew who was inside the club and were hoping for a photo-op...

Or, from the looks of the outfits of some of the girls standing outside the front doors where three large bouncers were keeping everyone back behind the velvet ropes, they were there in the hopes of a hookup. As I stepped out of the back of the cab after Natalie, I was shocked to see that some of them had signs that said "I Can Give You A Baby Shane! Drop The Wife And Come Be With A REAL Woman!"

I actually felt sick after reading that trash. I wasn't sure how the news that Harper couldn't have a baby had gotten out, but it had hit the tabloids a few weeks ago following a doctor's visit Shane and Harper had had with a specialist in fertility in Germany. I knew exactly when Natalie got a look at the sign because she approached the burly bouncers with her body nearly shaking with outrage.

"You get those bitches out of here before my brother sees them and commits murder," she commanded. "If anyone shows up with anything—ANYTHING—like that you get them a cab and send them to the other side of the city. Understand?"

The middle bouncer simply nodded while the one on the right moved forward to follow her orders. I rolled my eyes when the three chicks that had been holding the signs started protesting as they were led away. I wasn't a violent person, but I would have taken pleasure in getting to slap those three idiots a few times. Harper was a sweet girl and the fact that she couldn't have a baby was killing her.

After throwing out a few more commands, Natalie opened the door to the club and I followed her inside. "Motherfucking bitches," she kept muttering under her breath.

I bit my lip. "Do you think that anyone else saw that?"

"I know that Emmie didn't, because they were still standing there. And I know that Shane hadn't, because they were still breathing." Natalie handed her purse over to the coat check girl then offered the girl mine. "So either they aren't here yet, or those idiots haven't been there very long."

I glanced at the watch on my wrist and figured that it was the latter considering that we were running late for dinner by more than an hour. It was my fault that we were late. I'd wanted to do a few things before I had to face everyone—well, someone. A haircut wasn't something that was going to change me drastically because I simply refused to chop off my hair like Natalie had done. Although I was glad I had been able to talk her out of actually shaving her head, but the haircut she had decided on was not far off. She was rocking the pixie cut that some French guy with a lot of attitude had given her.

The new hairstyle looked cute on her, but I was mourning her hair for her.

I'd figured if she was going to change something about herself so that she could feel like she was putting the past behind her and moving forward with her life, then I needed to do something dramatic like that too. Getting my nose pierced was about as rebel as I was going though, because my nose was sore as hell right now. Still, I thought the stud in my nose was hot and worth the nose bleed I'd had for a few minutes afterwards.

The new piercing—fine, my only piercing other than my ears—along with my new outfit gave me a new confidence that I was planning on rocking tonight.

As we turned toward the bar where music was playing but at a moderate level compared to what it would have been if the place had been open to the public tonight, Natalie ran her fingers over her hair again. At least she had donated her hair to Locks of Love once I'd explained to her what it was, which made me feel a little less sad since her hair was going to a good cause. I'd never wanted a wig when I'd lost all my hair after chemo, but I was sure there were some little girls out there that would be happy to have one made out of Natalie Stevenson's glorious hair.

"How do I look?" Nat asked me nervously.

I let my eyes rove over her from head to toe. The haircut made her blue-gray eyes pop out more and actually highlighted her soft, feminine features. The new silver dress she had bought after trying on the entire store hugged her slight curves. The killer heels that we had shopped for longer than the actual dress, made her legs look longer. "You'll make him sweat, sweetie."

Her eyes darkened for a moment before she smiled. "Thanks. And I know that Wroth will lose his mind when he gets a look at you in that outfit."

I glanced down at my knee-high stiletto boots over black leggings that I was wearing under the short sleeved, yellow sweater dress that both hugged and hid my very, very curvy body. I wasn't tiny by anyone's standards, which I knew for a fact. But the added weight that I couldn't get rid of no matter how hard I tried because of my stupid thyroid didn't bother me all that much—

with a few exceptions. I preferred this body to the skeleton I'd been after my battle with cancer.

"Okay, let's get this over with," Natalie grumbled, turning and leading the way toward the distant sound of talking, laughter and music.

As we entered the bar, I took most of the room in all at once. The bar top was loaded down with a buffet of foods: prime rib, French fries, green beans, mac and cheese, salad, grilled chicken breasts, and even an assortment of desserts. The delicious smells caused my stomach to growl and I realized that with all the running around today that Natalie had to do, followed by our little makeovers, we hadn't had time to stop and have lunch.

My gaze shifted from the food to the rest of the room in the blink of an eye and I saw four different bands scattered around the room along with an array of children that ranged from the ages of sixteen to less than a year old. Lucy Thornton was sitting at a table in the back of the room with Harris Cutter, glasses of soda in their hands as they sat talking and laughing. Axton was standing with Nik Armstrong and two members of Alchemy, I couldn't remember either men's names. Drake Stevenson was sitting at a table with Liam and Linc while he held his sleeping daughter against his chest.

Two little boys that shouldn't have been as big as they were since they had been preemies toddled back and forward under the feet of their parents and loving family members. My heart melted at the sight of Luca and Lyric Thornton getting into mischief. Those two little monsters were the image of their father and left me aching for one of my own. Layla was keeping a keen eye on them, but the room appeared to have been baby proofed for tonight.

Emmie Armstrong, with a drink in one hand and her son hanging off her hip noticed us as we entered the room and nearly spit out her mouthful of soda when her green eyes landed on Natalie's hair. Those big green orbs widened and she pushed her son into the arms of his waiting nanny before rushing forward.

"Holy shit," Emmie murmured as she took hold of Natalie's arms. "What the hell happened to you?"

Natalie shrugged. "I needed a change."

"So you lost your mind and chopped off a part of yourself? Gee, way to follow the example of every other heartbroken chick in the world." Emmie glanced behind her, making sure that no one else had seen us yet, before turning back to her assistant. "Do you honestly think that your brother's won't ask questions now that you've done something like this? They've already been suspicious after the fall tour and the way you kept avoiding the OtherWorld bus and both Devlin and Zander. I'm not going to be able to keep them from questioning your sudden need to shed your freaking hair."

"I wasn't thinking about my brothers when I decided to cut my hair," Natalie muttered. "I just wanted to get rid of my hair. It was too much of a reminder…" She broke off and clenched her jaw.

Emmie's face softened for a moment. "I can understand that. Just be prepared to field questions from Drake and Shane... And try to act like being around Devlin and Zander doesn't make you want to stab one in the eye and cut the other's dick off."

A small giggle escaped me, because honestly that was exactly how Natalie felt when she was around both men. But Emmie had a point. Natalie had made it plain that she didn't want her brothers to know about the reasons why she now hated two of their friends with a burning passion that she had once loved Devlin Cutter with. She hadn't wanted her brothers to have a falling out with the two men and had sworn everyone to secrecy. The only reason that Emmie even knew was because she had been unable to keep her boss out of the loop once Devlin and Zander had trashed a club when the proverbial shit had hit the fan, leaving Zander with cracked ribs and Devlin with a concussion.

Natalie blew out a long sigh and nodded her head. "Okay. I'll try."

"Good." Emmie gave her arms a little squeeze before turning to greet me. "Fuck, you look beautiful. I'm digging that nose ring. When did you get that?"

"About forty-five minutes ago," I told her with a tight smile. "Figured it was time to get rid of at least one of my virginities." Next I was going to get a tattoo so that I no longer had virgin skin, and then that would leave me with only one virginity left. You know, the one that girls my age didn't have. The one that Wroth Niall had point blank told me he hadn't wanted before he'd gone and screwed some slut.

CHAPTER 4

WROTH

The room was loud with laughter, talking and music and I heard none of it. I was trapped in my own thoughts, my own misery. My self-hate.

I didn't want to be here, didn't want to be going back on tour in just a few days. I'd much rather be back in Tennessee working on the farm, hiding away from the world. That wasn't possible though. Not because of the band—fuck the band. They would be just fine without me. Unfortunately, I needed the band.

The band was my last connection to *her*.

Damn, I was pathetic. And an idiot. A stupid, pathetic idiot. Over the last year I'd done nothing but make one mistake after the other with the only person who has ever—ever—meant anything to me. Since Marissa had left me, walked away and never looked back, I've been in a dark place. Darker than I had ever been when I'd first gotten home from my deployment in

Afghanistan when I was in the marines. At least back then, I'd had a sweet-faced, twelve-year-old Marissa to come home to. Now I just had a house that was empty of the sunshine she had always brought to it, a heart that felt dead.

Scrubbing a hand over my face, I just barely refrained from cursing aloud, knowing that all the mothers in the room would make their husbands kick my ass if not actually do it themselves. When a nineteen-month-old pair of identical monsters walked by my table that no one else had seemed brave enough to approach in the last hour, I forced back my tormented thoughts and an involuntary smile broke free for the twin that was now trying to climb up my leg.

I haven't been around Jesse's boys very much, so I had no idea which was which. Their mother dressed them as differently as possible so that people who didn't see the twins on a regular basis could tell them apart, but I still had no clue which one was determined to now sit on my lap. Helping the kid out, I carefully lifted him the rest of the way up and placed him on my lap, facing me. "What's your name, kid?"

"That's Luca," a pregnant Lana murmured with a smile as she passed me with a plate of food in her hands. "Be careful with that one, Wroth. He's trouble."

I raised a brow at the kid who glanced up at his aunt as if she had just revealed government secrets. Laughing, she paused long enough to brush a kiss over the top of Luca's head before heading on her way. Once Lana was out of his

45

sight, Luca turned his full attention back to me. "So, you're the trouble maker?" Luca gave me a toothy grin and grabbed my shirt with both little fat hands before pulling himself into a standing position. I had very little experience with kids of any age so I had no idea what I was doing, but instinct took over and I held onto the little guy's waist as he released my shirt and started jabbering like we were old friends. When I felt a tug on my pants leg I found another little monster trying to climb my leg, wanting in on whatever fun his brother was having.

Laughing for what felt like the first time in a century, I lifted the second twin onto my lap and they both stood there jabbering at me, nodding their heads, and giving me grins that produced an outrageous amount of drool. I had no idea what either kid was talking about, but assumed it was about their adventures thus far in their young lives.

"Never thought I would see the day when Wroth Niall had a kid in his arms, let alone two."

My head snapped up at the sound of Jesse Thornton's deep chuckle. The twins' attention went straight to their father, and after only a small hesitation the second twin—Lyric, I remember his name being from when the kid was first born—held his hands out for Jesse. Luca, however, gripped my shirt tighter. Jesse lifted his son into his arms, still grinning down at me. "But at least my boys were able to make you look less like some homicidal maniac. Seriously man, you were scaring the shit out of me for a little while there. You need to relax before you have a stroke or something, dude."

I grunted, knowing that Jesse wasn't kidding about the scary way I was looking tonight. I knew that I was a scary looking man, with a voice that made most little kids cry. Which was why I'd been so surprised to have the twins want to approach me let alone want me to hold and talk to them. Of course, they looked kind of fearless. Meaning they had bigger balls than the men that worked on my farm back in Tennessee. These days even my foreman ran the other way when he saw me coming. I'd been moody, and a moody me was not something that people enjoyed.

The only person who had ever been able to handle me in a bad mood had washed her hands of me almost fourteen months ago.

And she was now standing less than a hundred feet from me, talking with Layla Thornton, Emmie, and some short-haired brunette who looked familiar but I didn't care enough to try and place. My next breath didn't come. It was trapped in my chest as I took in the sight of Marissa for the first time in what felt like a millennium.

Her long, glorious hair still hung past her waist, but it was styled in glossy waves. She was wearing more makeup than I'd ever seen on that beautiful face that haunted my dreams. A tiny diamond glinted from her nose and I clenched my jaw when I realized that she had gotten it pierced. It was a cute piercing on a chick, but on Marissa it pissed me off. I didn't want her pierced or tatted up. Not my Marissa. She was too damn pure to defile her body with holes and ink.

Someone must have said something funny, because Marissa's head suddenly was tossed back and she was laughing. It wasn't the laugh I was used to, the one that was full of joy and life, but it was enough to make my chest burn and my dick twitch in response to that musical sound. Fuck, but I'd missed her so much. My heart and my head had been fighting a losing battle for the last year and I was still no closer to figuring out how to deal with the conflict inside of me.

I loved Marissa Bryant. Have loved her every day of her life. In the beginning it had been a brother-like love for the six-year-old little girl who had come to live with me and my parents after the death of Brock Bryant. She had been so lonely, so lost since the only parent she had ever known was gone. When she had attached herself to my seventeen-year-old self, I'd let her. When the farm had nearly gone under because my father hadn't been able to keep up with the mortgage payments, I had joined the marines for the sign-on bonus just so I could help my parents keep a roof over Marissa's head.

I'd spent four years in the marines, three of which were in Afghanistan, for her. When I'd gotten home and joined OtherWorld I hadn't ever thought that the band would become what it was today. When Rich Branson had told us we had a shot at the big times, I hadn't wanted to be a part of it. Marissa had been twelve and I'd wanted to stay close, to protect her, but thankfully I'd followed my friends into the lime light and OtherWorld really had become as huge as Rich had predicted. It was the money OtherWorld produced that had allowed Liam and me to pay for the expensive medical treatment that Marissa had needed when we found out she had had leukemia when she was fourteen. Our fame had gotten her the treatment and eventually found the bone marrow donor that had saved her life.

That girl had been my best friend and I'd been terrified that I was going to lose her as I'd watched her fade away into nothing after the intense chemo treatments that had killed off everything bad inside of her before the doctors had done the bone marrow transplant. She might have only been sixteen, but she had gotten me like no one else ever had. Not even my mother had touched my soul like Marissa had then. She still did.

It wasn't until she was nineteen that my feelings had changed. One day I looked at Marissa and saw the same girl I'd always seen. The beautiful chick that could make me laugh when no one else could, with her kind blue eyes and slightly plump body. The next day? I'd seen the same chick, but just the sight of her had made me ache in a way I'd never ached before. I'd looked into her blue eyes, twinkling with merriment over something she was teasing me about, and had had a pain sharp and burning shoot through my chest, leaving me gasping for a breath that I still couldn't fully take in.

Ever since that day I'd had an inner struggle. My heart constantly screaming at me that Marissa was mine; that she needed to be beside me, in my arms. It was my head that I'd been listening to, however. My head that screamed and yelled and demanded I listen every second of every day. Marissa was innocent, her soul pure and beautiful. But I wasn't anywhere close to good enough for that girl. I'd done things in my life that would taint that pureness. I would infect her with my dirtiness, the evil that I'd seen and done while I was in the marines.

It was my heart that had overrode my head more than a year ago when I'd finally given in and kissed Marissa. A kiss wasn't anything major, not when you considered the things I've done with other women. But when a kiss burns through you to your heart and makes something inside of you come alive for the first time in your existence, then a kiss is everything. Everything. One kiss had led to another, and kissing had turned into all kinds of hot and crazy. How I'd been able to contain myself and not take something I wasn't good enough to have, I'll never be able to figure out.

I'd been struggling more and more with my feelings for Marissa ever since Liam's accident. As much as I babied and protected Marissa, she was pretty self-reliant and had never fallen apart over anything. Even when she was so sick, so close to death herself, she had been the strong one out of everyone. She'd stood strong while Liam had turned to harder and harder drugs to numb his pain. My mother had suffered a heart attack during those weeks that we couldn't see Marissa, something my father had died from just before Marissa had gotten so sick. And me? I'd been a basket case. A scary, moody basket case because Marissa was perhaps the only real friend who I've ever known and I'd felt like I was losing her every time I'd gone to that stupid window and looked at her sleeping form.

When Liam had the car wreck and we all thought that he might not make it, Marissa had practically collapsed. I'd never seen her so distraught in my life, and it woke up all my protective instincts. I didn't leave her side for days. When Liam finally woke up, and we went back to Liam's apartment to crash, Marissa had climbed into bed with me and fallen asleep in my arms. If I hadn't been so exhausted myself I would have stayed awake and savored the feeling of her in my arms, but after only a few hours of real sleep in over a week, I'd been unable to keep my eyes open when I was so at peace and the next thing I'd known it was morning.

We slept like that for several more days until we were positive that Liam was out of the woods. I wasn't surprised when Marissa decided to sleep in her own bed again, but I was definitely disappointed. Which told me that I was getting too close. If I got addicted to having her in my arms, then it was only going to worsen and my need for her would turn into an obsession.

After returning to Tennessee, I attempted to distance myself from her, but that wasn't easy. I hated being away from her for more than a few hours. When I wasn't touring with OtherWorld, I spent my evenings with Marissa either watching movies or just talking before bed. Simple things that didn't mean much to most folks, but meant the world to me and kept my head from exploding with images from my past. Marissa kept my demons quiet, soothed my pain and regret of things I'd done while in the marines.

In the end I ended up seeking her out more often than staying away, so much so that I ended up spending more time in her company than I would have normally. That should have told me I was getting weaker where she was concerned, but I'd ignored all signs.

The night of our first concert was where my heart overruled my head and let my natural instincts take over. Those instincts that told a man to take what was his, brand it, tell the world that it—she—was yours and yours alone...

The music was blaring throughout the club. It was just me and Axton in the VIP room. Zander was off hooking up, and Liam and Devlin had stayed on the bus. I kept thinking I should have stayed on the bus too, talked Marissa out of coming and made an early night of it. But she had wanted to come and since Devlin was staying on the bus there was no need for her to be there to watch out for Harris. If she was going to a club then I had to go. No way was I going to let her go out without me. Who would protect her from all those pricks that would want to seduce her?

Not long after we had arrived at the club, Marissa had talked Dallas into dancing with her and the two chicks had disappeared into the crowd downstairs. I'd wanted to object, but Marissa had been having fun and I didn't want to ruin that for her. It wasn't often Marissa got to hang out with other women, and I trusted Dallas. She was not only smoking hot, but able to take care of herself. She would protect Marissa if anything happened.

I was just finishing the last of my first beer when Marissa and Dallas walked into the VIP room. I hadn't consciously kept tabs on how long they were gone, but I'd counted the songs and they'd been down there dancing to four. Axton put his phone away as soon as Dallas and Marissa sat down beside us on the huge couch. Natalie had arranged for our group to be the only ones in the VIP room that night so the room felt empty with just the four of us in there.

Marissa picked up her glass of white wine, taking a thirsty swallow before fanning her sweat-damp face. "That was fun."

"You'll have to ask my date." I thought I heard Dallas say.

"What the fuck?"

I turned my head at Axton's growl with a frown. Axton was normally the laid back one of the five of us, but when it came to Dallas he was anything but his normal self. She brought out a fierceness in the rock star that resembled my own for Marissa. Lucky bastard could act on his *feelings though, while I was trapped in my own head with my feelings for my girl.*

Dallas giggled and picked up Marissa's hand. "I told you, she's my girl tonight." She lifted Marissa's hand and nibbled on her fingers, wiggling her brow at Marissa suggestively.

She meant to tease Axton, which from the sound of his tortured groan, he was. But the sight of her sucking on Marissa's finger, something I'd been fantasizing about just the night before when she had licked a smear of chocolate off her fingers made my jeans suddenly unbearably tight. Up until that moment I didn't think my dick had ever been so hard in my entire life. The groan that escaped me was strangled from my throat and I clenched my jaw before another sound could escape.

Marissa giggled and pulled her hand away. "Go on, Dallas. Have fun. I'm going to sit here and try to talk Wroth into ordering me something a little stronger than wine."

Axton stood, holding his hand out for Dallas, but his eyes were on mine. I put everything I had into that one look, practically begging my friend and bandmate not to leave me. I was almost to the point of no return from simply watching Dallas teasingly suck on Marissa's fingers. How the fuck was I supposed to keep my hands off her if they left me?

The fucking bastard gave me a grimace that said he was sorry, but he wasn't going to help me out. He tightened his hand around Dallas's fingers and pulled her out the door. Leaving me trapped with the star of all my wet dreams for the last four years.

Fucking hell.

Marissa turned her smiling face up to me. "Well, how about it?"

My throbbing dick twitched against the material of my jeans. "How about what?" I choked out.

She laughed. "How about ordering me something stronger than wine? Dallas's rum punch looked refreshing and I'm thirsty."

The thing about Marissa was that she was a light weight when it came to alcohol. She didn't do things that were going to mess with her decision making skills. Especially after watching what drugs had done to her brother. She drank a glass of wine every now and then but never more than one glass. "Rum is a hell of a lot stronger than wine, Mari."

Her eyes lit up when I used that particular nickname that only I had ever called her. I knew she loved it when I called her that and only used it when I wanted her to give in to whatever I was trying to persuade her to do. Of course there were times that that name slipped out, but now was not one of those times. I needed her as sober as possible if I was going to keep my hands off her.

"I'm aware of that, Wroth," she assured me with a smile. "But I want to relax a little more. And you're here in case I do something stupid. I trust you." She rested her head on my shoulder and gazed up at me from under her lashes. Those

long, thick, dark lashes. Surrounding the bluest eyes the world had ever seen.

Did she know what she did to me? Did she even know that she could do this to me? Make my body ache and my chest burn with a need that was all consuming. Or was she completely clueless to how much I wanted her, how much I loved and adored her?

When the door opened I nearly jumped out of my skin, feeling like I was a kid caught by my mother about to make out with my first girl. Looking up I saw that it was a waiter, bringing in more bottles of beer and water. I snatched another beer off the man's try before he had a chance to place them on the table in front of us.

"Can I get you anything else?" the man asked, glancing from me to Marissa. When his eyes landed on Marissa they lit up with interest that he quickly masked when I growled.

If Marissa heard my growl she didn't let on. Instead she smiled up at the waiter. "I'll have a rum punch, please."

I sighed, knowing she was going to get what she wanted regardless. "Top shelf," I told the waiter, making sure that Marissa would enjoy her drink as much as possible. If she was going to try rum, then it was going to be the best rum. Not that cheap ass shit that bars and clubs used unless you specified it.

"Right away," the waiter promised with a smile.

As soon as the door closed behind the man, I turned to face Marissa. "Is that dress new?"

She glanced down at her mid-thigh length gray dress. It had some kind of glittery shit on it, but it didn't rub off, thank fuck. I hated glitter. It got on everything and no matter how hard or long you rubbed, it never freaking came off. "I ordered it a few weeks ago. With all the clubs and after parties you guys do while on tour I figured I'd need some new things. Do you like it?"

Did I like it? I fucking hated it. The thing hugged her luscious curves like a glove. The top was low cut and whatever bra she was wearing pushed her beautiful tits up, making them look like they might spill out of her dress with one wrong move. The bottom ended at mid-thigh when she was standing, but with her sitting, it hiked up a good two inches. If she didn't have her legs tightly closed I would have gotten an eyeful of what color her panties were.

I wasn't used to seeing her in sexy clothes like this. She normally wore jeans and T-shirts on the farm. If we happened to have to attend something that required she dress up, Marissa always wore things that were demure, almost conservative. Wanting to hide her lusciousness rather than show it off. What the fuck was she doing showing it off now?

"Wroth?" She said my name with a small laugh that didn't mask her hurt feelings.

I bit back a curse. Hurting Marissa was like hurting myself. I hated hurting her feelings, but it was more than obvious I'd done so when I hadn't answered her right away. "It's beautiful, Mari. But nowhere near as beautiful as you."

Her eyes widened, as if she were surprised at my answer. "Really?"

Without thinking about what I was doing I lifted a hand and pushed a few strands of her long, glossy hair back behind her ear. "Really."

Her hand caught mine and held it against her cheek for a moment. "You're so sweet at times, Wroth Niall." She grinned up at me, her eyes looking mischievous. "It's kind of cute."

"Are you saying I'm cute, Mari?" I took a long pull from the bottle of beer. It was some kind of imported shit, something I hated, but it tasted good enough.

Even in the dim lighting of the VIP room, I could still see the pink that filled her cheeks. "You're a lot more than cute, Wroth. You know that you're sexy as sin. Sometimes I hate how good you look." She dropped my hand and glanced down at her nearly empty glass of wine. "I hate all those girls that chase you," she mumbled as if she were talking to herself.

I suddenly felt as if I couldn't breathe. Her words had been soft, but packed a punch so strong it had knocked the air from my lungs. The beer in my hand dropped to the floor beside the long couch with a crash, sending foamy liquid spraying across the carpeted floor. If it shattered I didn't know, because I was too busy pulling her onto my lap.

Grabbing hold of her long, nearly black hair I jerked her head back so that I could get a better view of those big blue eyes. "Repeat that," I commanded in a voice that was hoarse with a desire that was suddenly consuming every fiber of my being.

I felt her tremble but knew instinctively that it wasn't from fear. I have never given Marissa a reason to fear me. And I never would. Her eyes dilated, her tongue sneaking out to dampen her lips as she met my gaze brazenly. "I hate them," she told me with a flare to her nose that suggested she was jealous just thinking about some other chick chasing after me.

"No reason to hate them, girl." I wrapped her hair tighter, letting my gaze drift down her neck to the pulse beating rapidly at the base. It was faster than the tempo of the music that was vibrating the walls, keeping pace with the beat of my own heart that was pulsing in my dick. "None at all."

"There are plenty," Marissa snapped. "Especially when I see your hands on them. It makes me hate you just as much as I hate them."

If my heart was racing a second ago it was completely stopped at those words. Marissa hating me just wasn't something that I could handle. Ever. It made me crazy. Made the burning in my heart turn into an inferno. "Tell me not to touch them, Mari. Tell me and I won't."

Her eyes widened. "I don't believe you."

"Have I ever lied to you? Do you have any reason to not believe me?" My hand had wrapped her hair around my wrist until I was now cupping the back of her skull. I used my thumb to massage her scalp. "Tell me, Mari. Tell me."

"Don't touch them," she whispered, losing some of her confidence. Long, dark, thick lashes lowered to hide those blue eyes from me. Hiding her thoughts from me. "Please don't touch them, Wroth."

"Okay," I rasped. Pulling her head down, I nuzzled the side of her neck. "Anything you want, sweetheart. Anything at all. All you ever have to do is say the words." She should have already known that. Hadn't I proved to her that she meant everything to me? That all I wanted was her happiness?

"Kiss me," she whispered so softly that at first I wasn't sure I had heard her correctly.

"What?" I whispered back, enjoying the smell of whatever perfume she was wearing just under her left ear. Fuck, her skin was soft and smelled so delicious. I licked my dry lips and growled in pure pleasure as the tip skimmed over her delicate skin. That one tiny taste sent my body even harder and my hand tightened on her head as I attempted to gain some semblance of control over my wayward body.

The voice in my head, the one that constantly told me that I was no good for this girl, that I would only bring her heartache and taint her with the evilness that I had seen and performed while in the marines was quieter than usual. The voice of my heart, the one that always seemed so faint, was suddenly screaming to take what was mine. Love her, cherish her.

"Kiss me, Wroth," Marissa said just a fraction louder, but I heard her.

"Will that make you happy?" I found myself asking, like an idiot. Only a complete and total idiot would ask that stupid question. Of course it would make her happy. It would sure as fuck make me happy.

Her hands lifted to hold onto my shoulders. Her head lowering until her lips were just a few inches away from my own. "It would make me the happiest person in the world right now. I've wanted you to kiss me again since I was sixteen years old. Remember the night before that last chemo treatment and that kiss you gave me before the nurse tossed you out of my room that night?"

I closed my eyes as the memory of that innocent, sweet kiss rushed into my mind. That kiss had been nothing more than a kiss between friends. I'd been so scared that I would never see her again, hold her again, or make her laugh again. Marissa's plea for a kiss, her first kiss, had torn me apart and I'd readily obliged. That kiss didn't count as our first kiss though. I'd felt none of the desire that now boiled my blood to the point that I was about to combust on that leather couch.

"I've been dying for a real kiss from you, Wroth. If you say that I can have anything I ask for, then I'm asking for that. Kiss me." Her long nails bit into the muscles of my shoulder through my T-shirt. "Please..?"

If I'd been standing, that hesitantly murmured 'please' would have buckled my knees. A curse lifted to my lips, but died just as quickly as I pulled her those last few inches separating our lips. Her mouth opened in surprise and I took advantage, diving deep with my tongue to steal her taste like a thief. A thief that had been dying for a sip of her sweet, sweet taste. I invaded, stole every drop she had to give and then demanded more as I stroked my tongue with hers, tangling them together in the hopes that they tied into a knot and we would have to stay like that for the rest of our lives.

Marissa's whimper forced me to pull back, scared that I might have hurt her in my eagerness to finally—FINALLY—taste her. "Okay?"

"Yes. Don't stop." Her hands lifted from my shoulders only for her fingers to stab through my hair. Our teeth snapped together as she fused her mouth back to mine but I felt no pain as I got another taste of her intoxicating essence.

The longer we kissed, the harder my body seemed to throb, but I refused to go further. Not yet. Not tonight. This kiss was too good, too fucking perfect for me to dare destroy this memory with seducing her on the damn couch in some freaking club that we weren't likely to return to anytime soon. The hand wrapped around her hair stayed in place while my free one caressed up and down her spine. The feel of her trembling with each passing moment, the sound of her panting mingled with my own as we kissed, nipped at each other's lips with sharp teeth only to lick away any stings, was better than any sexual experience I'd ever had up until that point in my life.

The waiter returned and I opened my eyes to watch long enough as he put the drinks on the table and left again, not daring to break the kiss the entire time. Marissa hadn't heard the man, and I wasn't going to stop my little slice of heaven for his fucking ass.

The kiss continued until Marissa finally pulled back and rested her forehead against my own. Tomorrow her mouth was going to be raw and sore, but right then those luscious lips were plump and damp from my kisses. There had never been a sexier sight...

The memory of that first kiss haunted me repeatedly, replaying over and over again, taunting me with how earth shaking it had been. Still was.

The toddler in my arms suddenly protested and I forced my attention back onto the little guy in my arms. "Sorry, little dude." I placed a glaring Luca on his feet where his brother now was, their father having moved on since I'd been lost in my own thoughts. The two hugged like they hadn't seen each other in days rather than mere minutes and then rushed in the direction where their mother was still talking with Emmie, Marissa and the short-haired chick.

When the twins reached the four women, the short-haired chick crouched down and I realized that she was Natalie. My eyes widened, because I'd thought she was just as hung up on her hair as Marissa had always been on her own. I wouldn't say that this haircut looked bad on the chick, but it wasn't anything to be desired, either. At least not by me.

Natalie grabbed hold of Lyric and lifted him, kissing his cheek with loud smacking kisses that I heard all the way across the room. Wanting some new attention for himself, Luca grabbed hold of Marissa's dress and tugged until she bent to lift him into her arms. She gave the kid a kiss then rubbed her nose against his, making him giggle.

A reluctant smile lifted my lips at the sight of them together like that. Marissa was a natural with kids, and I knew she was going to make a great mother one day. All though it had been controversial at the time, Marissa had had eggs harvested and frozen so that she could have a chance at being a mother later in life if she ever decided that it was something that she wanted to do. She was lucky, because there were women out there who hadn't had that option before facing a round of chemo that would kill any chances of ever having a child of their own.

Layla said something that caught Marissa's attention and she lifted her head to reply. And just when I thought I liked Luca, he goes and pulls on the top of Marissa's dress exposing her beautiful, bra-covered tits to the entire room.

CHAPTER 5

MARISSA

Another giggle bubbled up at the same time I felt my face turning blood red. I quickly tried to pry my dress from Luca's beefy little fingers without much success.

"Oh my gods!" Layla sputtered embarrassedly. "Luca, that's naughty. Marissa, I'm so sorry."

I shook my head at her as I continued to try to cover my exposed chest and my new—very *sheer*—bra. "It's okay," I said and laughed. "I should have known better with this little man. Especially after last time." Last time it had been less embarrassing, because I'd had on a simple cotton bra that did not display my breasts in a way that I might as well not have even been wearing a bra.

Luca did not like me disrupting his fun. He grunted and whined as I carefully pulled his hands free and his mother quickly pulled him into her arms and started quietly scolding the tot.

Natalie and Emmie had moved to stand in front of me to offer me some privacy as I righted my dress top, but both were laughing so hard they were shaking. "Nice, you two. Real nice. I'm pretty sure that everyone in the room knows what color my nipples are right now, and all you two can do is giggle like pubescent juveniles."

"I saw that happening from a mile away," Emmie snorted through her laughter. "Luca really likes nice tits, Rissa. And they don't get any nicer than your rack, babe."

"Boys got some great taste," a new voice spoke up and my head snapped up from making sure that my top was covering everything that it needed to. When I saw Rhett Tomlinson standing behind Emmie I couldn't help but smile at the lead singer of Trance. The sexy as sin rocker had been a regular at our apartment lately and we'd become fast friends over the last several months.

"You're just biased." I pushed through my two friends to wrap my arms around Rhett's neck. "Where have you been hiding? I haven't seen you in over a week." I glanced at Natalie over my shoulder. "Have you been mean again, Nat? Stop scaring the guy away."

Natalie rolled her blue-gray eyes. "Yeah, it's my fault. Couldn't be anyone else that runs their mouth and pushes him out the door more often than not."

Turning back to the leanly muscled, sweat worthy hottie, I leaned up on the tip of my toes and kissed his cheek. "Ignore her. She doesn't know what she's talking about. It's the haircut, it did something to her brain when all that hair came off."

Rhett turned his head and brushed his lips across mine before shooting a mock glare at Natalie. "What the fuck were you thinking cutting off all that hair? Damn it, woman. I was half in love with you because of that hair alone."

"You're lucky I still have any hair." Natalie wiggled her brow at him, making him flash that sexy grin that would have affected a ninety-year-old woman. "I wanted to shave it, but Marissa talked me out of it. This was my compromise."

Rhett smacked his long fingered hand against my hip playfully, making me squeal in surprise. "Rissa, you should have called me. I would have come over and tied her to the bed so she couldn't leave the apartment." Dark chocolate eyes met mine and he winked before his gaze was attracted by my new facial accessory. "Holy shit, that's hot."

Delight filled me and I hugged him again. "Really? You like it?"

"Fuck yeah, I like it. You definitely should have called me when you decided to get that little baby. Would have loved to have seen that happen. When are you going to get your first tat? We're stopping in Miami in August. Tell me what you want and I'll talk to the guy that does all my ink there. We can set you up an appointment, make a date out of it."

Excitement made me giddy and I jumped up and down. I'd been thinking of getting a tattoo for a while now, but I wanted to be absolutely sure I was in love with whatever I decided on before getting it permanently inked into my skin. "That sounds like fun. Let me think about what I want first and I'll let you know."

"Let him know what?" Liam asked as he and Linc joined our group. His eyes narrowed on Rhett before pulling me into his arms and kissing my temple. "That piercing is adorable, Rissa."

"Adorable?" I glared up at him. "Adorable wasn't what I was going for, Li."

"Sure it is." Liam winked down at me. "Now, what do you need to let him know?"

"What tattoo I want."

"Marissa." Liam shook his head, then turned a cold glare on Rhett. "No. She doesn't need any ink."

"I want a tattoo, Liam." I pulled away from him and stepped back into Rhett's arms. "And it's not up to you whether I get one or not. My body, my choice."

"Rissa…" My brother let out a long sigh, but then perked up. "So does this mean you'll be going with me on tour?"

It was my turn to sigh. I'd been thinking about it hard all day, but hadn't made up my mind until Rhett had mentioned tattoos and Miami. "Looks like it."

Liam pulled me away from Rhett once more and swung me around and around, making me giggle and cling to his shoulders. My heart warmed at the happiness I saw in his eyes. Liam deserved happiness. When he put me on my feet again he surprised us all by shaking Rhett's hand.

"Guess I have to thank you for getting her to come. Even if it was with bribery of ink and debauchery."

Rhett put his hand in Liam's, grinning... until Liam's grip on his hand tightened painfully. Rhett's grin disappeared and his eyes widened ever so slightly. "There will be no debauchery, understand?"

"Liam!" I pushed his shoulder, making him drop Rhett's hand. Didn't Liam understand that Rhett and I were just friends? Rhett was fun to be around, great to talk to and I trusted him enough to confide in him. But he wasn't into me and I definitely wasn't into him. Not that I would ever explain that to my brother if he didn't already know that. I wasn't likely to explain it to anyone.

Emmie clapped her hands together. "I was hoping you would come with us. I love you to pieces, girl, but I also have ulterior motives. With all the kids with us on this tour, I was hoping to add you to my payroll as a helper for my nanny, Felicity."

"You don't have to pay me, Em," I assured her. "I love to help out."

"Hell yeah, I have to pay you. Have you ever been around all of these brats without their parents to run interference? Trust me, Ris. You will be begging me for double pay by the end of the tour."

"Okay, then." I hugged her. "Just let me know what I need to do and I'll take care of it."

"I'll email Natalie with all the paperwork to add you to the payroll. I'll have to get back to you on what bus you will be on. We still haven't worked out all the sleeping arrangements. Alchemy and Trance have one bus to share, but we're going to call that the party bus. As long as no one kills each other and there is no drug use I don't really care what goes on." Emmie shrugged. "Then there are the OtherWorld buses. One was turned into a private bus for Axton and Dallas. We revamped it. But the other one is the same as it was…" Her eyes drifted to someone behind me, but I didn't pay attention. With the room full of so many people it was hard to tell who she was focused on right then anyway. "Although I'm sure that isn't really an option for you. Still, the Demon's all have their own private buses so I'm sure we can fit you in somewhere."

"Seven buses? I'm sure that I'll find somewhere to call home for the next few months." I glanced up at Rhett, giving him a teasing look from under my lashes. "Wanna share a roost?"

"Oh, fuck," Natalie muttered under her breath, but she was standing so close I was able to catch it. I glanced at her, curious as to what had made her sound so stressed all of a sudden. She was looking at something past my shoulder too, and inquisitively I followed her gaze.

My heart completely stopped at the sight of the man standing just a few feet behind me. Damn it, why did he have to look so good? His jeans hung off his narrow waist, his shirt molded across a hard chest and sculpted abdomen. His hair was a little messy, as if he had been running his fingers through it… But it was his eyes, those espresso dark eyes that made me jerk back.

They were blazing with a rage that left me breathless. His gaze was locked onto Rhett as if he wanted to break every bone in his body. I had little hope that that wasn't the case. Jealously, pure and simple, was radiating through his rage, and I had two thoughts.

One, that I needed to save my friend from a date with death. And two…? That I wanted to kick Wroth Niall's ass because he had no right to be jealous of anyone I was or wasn't having a relationship with because he had lost all privileges to me and my life when he had cheated on me.

A growl came from Wroth and he took a step closer to me and Rhett. I started to get in between the two men when Linc and Natalie each took a hold of Rhett's arms. "I'm hungry, Rhett." Natalie told him with a beaming smile that almost hid her trepidation. "How about coming and eating with me? The buffet looks delicious."

Rhett pulled his arm free from Natalie only to wrap it around her shoulders as they walked off, Linc standing behind the two as the three of them walked off. I breathed a sigh of relief as they got out of harm's way, knowing that Wroth wouldn't have thought twice about killing someone when it came to me…

It was just too bad he hadn't thought about that when he broke my heart last year.

CHAPTER 6

WROTH

I'd been glued to my seat when Luca had pulled Marissa's top down, exposing those perfect tits to my eyes. Of course it had been to the eyes of every other fucker in the room as well. But I hadn't really thought too hard about that as I'd watched her work her clothes free of the little dude and pull her top up. I had even had a small grin on my face as Layla had walked by me, still gently scolding her son for being naughty.

That grin had completely disappeared as the lead singer for Trance, one of the two bands that were opening for us this summer, joined Marissa's small group. The way Marissa's blue eyes had lit up at the sight of the guy had been like a kick to my chest, knocking all the breath from my lungs as a mixture of emotions had started to simmer in my gut. But I'd locked my jaw and tried to get control of myself, thinking that I had no reason to feel the way I currently was from just a look in Marissa's eyes.

And then she had walked right into that douchebag's arms and kissed his cheek. Still nothing to worry about, I'd told myself as I'd taken a swallow of my iced tea making sure that I got a few ice cubes in the process. It was when that creep had turned his head and kissed My. Fucking. Girl. That wasn't when the rage had boiled over and I'd gotten to my feet. No, that had come when he had slapped her on the ass. *That* was when I'd seen red.

I'd taken slow steps toward the growing group, afraid I might destroy the entire room if I didn't walk slowly. With each step, my hands clenched into fists and then relaxed. My voice of reason was trying to calm me down, tell me that it had looked like an innocent enough kiss. There had been no lingering touches, their lips had been closed. Marissa hadn't clung to the guy. All of those things were in Rhett's favor.

By the time I got to Marissa's group she'd been joined by her brother and Linc. I liked Linc. It had made me sleep just a little easier at night knowing that that big muscle-headed fucker was watching over my Marissa. I was actually seeing a little more clearly by the time I stopped just a few feet behind Marissa…

"Wanna share a roost?" Marissa asked Rhett as she looked seductively up at the motherfucker.

My rage went from a low simmer to boiling over and catching fire. My voice of reason had been replaced with a voice that was shouting at me to kill. Kill. Kill that fucking bastard. Marissa was not one to openly flirt with a man. She did not tease or play sexual games with people. She was sweet, innocent. Pure. That she was doing the exact opposite with Rhett told me that Marissa was either sleeping with that dickhead or wasn't far from doing so.

And. I. Was. Going. To. Fucking. Destroy. Him.

"Back up, Wroth." Liam's voice broke through the white noise that was like static in my brain, torturing me until I destroyed Trance's lead singer. There was something dangerous in my cousin's voice and I turned my head so I could focus on the man.

The personal training had paid off, because Liam was twice the size he had been on Valentine's Day when I'd seen him last. Linc's hard workout regimen was keeping my cousin and bandmate clean so I would be eternally grateful for Linc. I loved Liam like a brother.

But that wasn't going to save him if he got in my way right now.

"What did you say?" I murmured.

"I said, back the fuck up. The room is full of little kids and every one of their fathers will hold you down and destroy you if you start a fight in front of their kids." His words made me able to rein in most of my control, but I still had murder on my mind. It wasn't the first time I'd killed a man, but it would be the first time I'd have done it with pleasure. Liam's next words, however, cooled my rage to a small simmer. "And you don't want to chance Marissa getting hurt, do you?"

My eyes snapped back to Marissa who was standing just a few feet away. I could reach out and pull her into my arms, hold her for the first time in a million years. I wanted to do it so fucking bad. But the way she was standing there, glaring at me with her own rage making her glorious body tremble, I knew that she would probably be the one to commit murder if I touched her.

"Mari…" She flinched at my use of the name only I have ever used. The sight of that flinch was like swallowing a glass of bleach, the effects were the same. My gut twisted in pain and my insides started to burn with poison. I cleared my throat because it was suddenly clogged with emotion. "Can we talk?"

"I have nothing to say to you." She clenched her hands into fists, and I wondered if she was imagining pounding them against my chest or maybe knocking my lights out with a punch to the jaw. I deserved both from her and would have welcomed the punishment if it meant that she would have forgiven me. "Except to tell you to stay the hell away from me."

She might as well have told me to stop breathing. I would have been able to do so for a few minutes, but then instinct would take over and I would breathe on my own. That was how it was when it came to her. I would try to go against nature and keep my distance, to protect her from all my stupid shit, but then instinct would take over and I would have to be close to her. I'd finally accepted that.

After I'd fucked up to the point that the woman who had once loved me just as much as I loved her, now hated the sight of me.

CHAPTER 7

MARISSA

I was still shaking with lingering rage as I tossed random foods onto a plate. The smell of the food didn't even register. It could have been sawdust for all I cared. Grabbing a bottle of Voss, I carried my dinner to the nearest table that had someone I didn't mind listening to talk while I stabbed at my food rather than eating it.

Luckily for me it was with Lana who was sitting with Harper, Dallas, and the lead singer of Alchemy, Bishop. They all smiled when I took the empty chair between Dallas and Harper. Dallas's smile turned into a frown when she saw that I wasn't smiling back. "What did he do this time?"

"Nothing," I told her, forcing a smile. "I don't want to talk about it," I rushed to tell her when she opened her mouth to call bullshit. "Where's Cannon?" I asked to distract her. All you ever had to do to change the subject with

Dallas or Axton Cage was to mention their adorable baby boy.

Dallas's face lit up and she glanced over her shoulder to where a playpen had been set up. "He's sleeping. I don't know how he can snooze through all these people talking, but he is his father's son."

"Drake says that Axton could sleep through a hurricane," Lana said with a laugh before taking a hearty bite of ribs smothered in BBQ sauce. She licked her lips, then started sucking on her thumb. Apparently when you were six months pregnant you had to make sure you got every last smear of whatever you were eating. "So I can get why Cannon would sleep through this craziness."

"Someone please distract my husband," Harper muttered as she glanced over my shoulder. She was frowning hard, and her jaw was clenched. "I have no idea what is going on with Nat, but she and Devlin are about to tear each other's hair out... Well, what's left of Nat's hair. Seriously, why would she cut it that short? I can just see how Stella is going to react when she drops Jenna off tomorrow."

Lana's eyes widened when she followed her sister-in-law's gaze. "Holy shit. I didn't even notice her. I thought she was just as obsessed with her hair as Drake is with his. Oh, damn. The Stevenson brothers just zeroed in on little sister drama." Lana scooted back her chair and stood as quickly as her ever growing belly would allow. "Harper, maybe you should try and talk your man into some bathroom action. He seems to like that shit so much it's liable to distract him for a good thirty minutes."

"And have Jesse's wrath rain down on my head?" Harper shook her head but followed Lana as they both went to catch their husbands before they could reach the very obvious arguing couple by the buffet.

Even from where I was sitting I could see the pain in Devlin's aquamarine eyes as he kept staring at Natalie's short hair. I'd thought that Natalie had cut her hair to make her feel like she was starting a new chapter in her life. Now, I could tell that she had done it just to punish Devlin Cutter. I didn't really blame her for wanting to hurt him over and over again, because yeah, she'd been doing plenty of that. Maybe she hadn't gone out and started sleeping around to get back at him, but she'd sure as hell made statements with some of the things she'd done in the last year or so. Not that I was taking up for Devlin, because I wouldn't do that. Not when he had basically shattered Natalie to the point of no return. But that didn't mean I liked to watch him being in pain.

Looking away, Dallas and I locked gazes and shared a knowing look. Other than Emmie, we were the only women who knew what was really going on with Natalie because she had sworn us all to secrecy. Drake and Shane were close with both Devlin and Zander and if the Stevenson brothers found out what had happened last spring then it would be the end of those friendships... And Devlin's and Zander's lives. That Natalie cared enough about saving their sorry skin, had to mean she must still care about both a lot.

Before everything had turned sour last year, Natalie and Zander had been good friends, but friends was all it was ever going to be because Natalie was blind to anyone but Devlin. Zander, however, hadn't been able to accept that and had made the bet with Devlin. And when it looked like Devlin had won that stupid bet, Zander had ruined Devlin's relationship with Natalie by spilling the beans about the bet.

Glancing back toward the buffet where Devlin and Natalie were still having a whispered argument, I saw that Lana had easily distracted Drake. He was now wrapped around his wife with his hands rubbing over her distended belly where yet another daughter was growing. Lana murmured something that had the big man laughing, his blue-gray eyes sparkling with happiness. I could remember a time when Drake rarely laughed, when his eyes were bloodshot and almost yellow because of all the Jack Daniels he consumed on a daily basis. It melted my heart to see how happy he was now, to see his eyes clear and alight with peace that his little family had brought him.

Harper had locked onto Shane, and was standing on tiptoes to whisper in her husband's ear. He was grinning and nodding his head, but his eyes kept straying toward his sister every few seconds. The smile would dim until Harper would whisper something else. After a moment she started tugging on his hand, leading him toward the back where the bathrooms were. Obviously Lana's suggestion had worked...

"You think this is easy for me, Nat?" Devlin suddenly demanded loud enough for the entire room to hear him. "Well, it's fucking not."

Shane froze and shot around to glare at the man talking to his sister across the room. Harper grabbed onto his arm tighter. "Leave it alone, Shane," she told him but he extracted his arm carefully so he wouldn't hurt her then started toward his sister. "She can handle it."

Drake's attention had also been caught and his head snapped up at the sound of Devlin talking the way he had to his sister. Drake and Shane might not have had anything to do with their sisters growing up, but as soon as Jenna and Natalie had come back into their lives they had more than made up for the brotherly love and protectiveness.

As the two brothers quickly gained ground between the OtherWorld drummer and their sister, I pictured the entire room turning into a blood bath that would really screw up the peace of the upcoming tour. I bit my lip, suddenly wanting to hide under the table.

Dallas stood up so quickly I didn't have time to blink. "Hey, Axton and I wanted to share our news with y'all," she informed the room at large, practically yelling the words.

It worked because Shane and Drake paused to look at her. Even Devlin and Natalie were distracted by her so that they turned to face her. Dallas glanced around for Axton who was frowning at his wife. "We do?" he said as he sat down his glass of tea and crossed to her. "I thought we weren't going to say anything right now."

"Now's as good as any, babe." She gave him a tight smile. "It's okay. We wouldn't have been able to keep it a secret for much longer anyway."

Axton rolled his hazel eyes. "Fine. Okay."

"What's going on?" Emmie demanded as she and Nik stepped forward, her son hanging off her hip once again. Jagger was such a momma's boy. "What? Are you two..?" Her eyes widened as a look passed between her and Axton. "No. No way."

"Yes." Axton nodded, a huge smug grin splitting his face. "Dallas and I are pregnant again. Baby number two will be here the first week of December."

The room erupted with cheers and congratulations. Nik shook Axton's hand and Emmie hugged Dallas, both of them laughing. I was stunned because Dallas and Axton's son had just been born in February. It was now the end of May. They hadn't waited long to start back at it like rabbits, that was for sure. Laughing, I stood to hug the couple. Dallas's arms tightened around me as she glanced at something over my shoulder, and I knew who she was looking at.

Harper.

When I turned I couldn't help but bite my lip at the flash of pain that crossed Harper's gorgeous face for a moment, only to be quickly replaced by a huge grin just before she tossed her arms around her best friend. "You dirty whore," Harper said and laughed as she hugged Dallas tightly. "Did you even wait until the doctors gave the okay, or were you spreading your legs the first night you got home from the hospital?"

"Shut up, bitch," Dallas snickered as the two danced around while continuing to hug each other for another moment. But then Dallas's grin faltered and she stepped back from her friend. "I'm sorry, Harp."

"Stop." Harper shook her head, stopping whatever apology Dallas had been about to make. "Just because I can't have a baby doesn't mean that you need to feel bad about being pregnant. Don't let my hang-ups put a damper on what should be a happy time for you and Axton. I'm so excited for you, Dallas... Do I get to be godmother again?"

"We wouldn't want anyone else, Harper," Axton assured her as he wrapped his arm around his wife's still tiny waist.

I glanced away from them, blinking back tears. Harper Stevenson was truly the strongest person I knew. Bishop, who'd been sitting there watching the whole scene with guarded eyes, caught my gaze. Seeing my tears he grunted and handed me his napkin. I'd only met the grumpy-looking singer a few times, but he'd always been nice to me. He seemed like a private person, with little sign of a sense of humor. Bishop reminded me of Wroth in those regards, so it was little wonder that I found him curious.

"You okay?"

I offered him a small, teary smile. "Yeah, I'm good. Just get a little weepy from time to time." I lifted my bottle of Voss to my lips and took a small sip of the water. "How have you been, Bishop?"

The man shrugged and I took a moment to glance over what I could see of him since we were sitting on opposite sides of the table. He wasn't conventionally handsome; his face was more often than not expressionless, and his features were on the plain side. His body was lean—very lean—with only a few muscles here and there with little definition. But it wasn't his looks that got him noticed. It was his freaking voice, and the way he brought a song to life with each word he sang.

I knew for a fact he wasn't skinny because of drugs. Since Emmie had signed on as both Trance and Alchemy's manager she did monthly drug tests. It was her stipulation for every member of every band she managed. I was pretty sure she did it so that it didn't hurt Liam's feelings so badly since she wanted to keep a close eye on his continued recovery, but also because she didn't really know or trust the two new bands she was dealt with. Drug addicts were liabilities and Emmie had a new and quickly rising reputation to uphold.

"I can't complain," Bishop finally said after a moment or so of silence. "How about you, beautiful?"

I felt my cheeks fill with pink when he called me beautiful. I wasn't used to men calling me that. At least not very often. Wroth had on a few occasions, but they had been so rare that each one of them had felt like a caress. At the thought of Wroth, my eyes unconsciously moved through the room until I found him standing against a wall with his hands thrust into his pockets. His dark gaze was glaring up at the ceiling, his jaw clenched as if he were still mad. No doubt he probably was. It was hard to get Wroth's anger to completely evaporate unless I was there to soothe his ruffled feathers.

He must have felt my gaze on him because his gaze slowly lowered and then locked on me. My heart clenched and I boldly held his gaze for a moment before finally, out of self-preservation, lowered my eyes. Memories of a time when I thought my world couldn't be more perfect flashed through my mind, pausing for a moment on one of my favorite memories…

The day after the Panama show, after the night I'd gotten the first true kiss of my adult life, found me exhausted. I hadn't slept for more than a few hours on the bus. My mind had refused to shut down as I had gone over every last detail of that kiss a million times. Damn, but Wroth Niall had blown my mind with that kiss and every kiss that had quickly followed.

My mind was still on that kiss as I walked into my hotel room to discover it was a suite with two bedrooms. I hadn't been paying attention when Natalie had passed out room keys, my mind still stuck on last night. But as soon as I realized that I was going to be sharing a room, I'd known who my roommate was going to be. Wroth wasn't going to let anyone else bunk with me. He was too overprotective.

With my heart beat suddenly racing at the thought of sharing the suite with the man I could still taste on my tongue, I moved through the sitting area of the room and took a seat on the long couch in front of the flat screen. From one of the two bedrooms I could hear the water already running from Wroth's shower. My exhaustion was surprisingly gone now and I felt wired, as if I'd drunk too much Monster.

"Rissa?"

I glanced up at the sound of my name coming from that rough voice. "Hi," I greeted him, feeling surprisingly shy all of a sudden.

Dark espresso eyes skimmed over me from head to toe and it felt as if he had physically touched me the way my skin seemed to suddenly bead with goose bumps and I was unable to repress a shiver. My own eyes were doing some traveling of their own. I'd expected his hair to be wet since I'd heard water running, but it wasn't. He was still wearing the jeans and T-shirt I'd seen him wearing earlier, both of which fit him perfectly. The T-shirt was stretched over the wide, hard planes of his chest. The jeans hanging slightly off his hips, giving just a tease of a glance of tanned flesh between the hem of his shirt and the top of his old jeans.

"I'm running you a bath, sweetheart." He crossed to the couch and offered me his hand.

Running me a bath? Oh goodness! I bit my lip, trying to hide my excitement and the way his words had made my heart melt as I put my hand in his big rough one. Long fingers wrapped around my hand, trapping it in his, and he gave a small tug, urging me up. Without a word I let him lead me into what must have been the master bedroom and into the connecting bathroom.

The scent of warm vanilla and honey filled the room as the huge bathtub filled with bubbles came into view. When we reached the side of the tub, Wroth released my hand and turned off the water. When he straightened, he caught me around the waist and pulled me against his hard body. Before I could guess at his intentions, he lowered his head and brushed a soft kiss over my parted lips. Tears burned my eyes at his gentleness. I'd never seen him be this tender in all the years I'd known Wroth. That he was being this way with me didn't surprise me, but it did make me fall a little deeper for him.

"Take your bath, sweetheart. I'm going to order us an early dinner and we can relax for a few hours before we have to head over for tonight's show." His nose nuzzled against my ear, making me tremble with a desire that was starting to incinerate my body from the inside out.

With another soft kiss to my lips, he left me alone in the bathroom. I stood there for a long moment, still savoring the feel of his lips on mine. Without even realizing what I was doing, I lifted my fingers to skim across the slight dampness from his kiss, massaging his essence into them. For several minutes I stood like that, until with a happy giggle I started taking my clothes off.

Sliding into the water was pure nirvana. The water temperature was perfect. Not so hot that it would burn, but just enough to release all the tense muscles that had bunched up over the last few days. The sweet smell of the bubble bath relaxed me further and I dunked my head under the water, enjoying the bath like a little girl might for just a moment.

Lifting my head, I smoothed my wet hair back from my face and wiped water from my eyes. When I could see again, I gasped at the sight standing in front of me. Wroth had returned from ordering room service and had gotten rid of most of his clothes. His boots, socks, jeans and shirt were gone, leaving him standing in front of me in nothing but a pair of black Hanes boxers. Damn, but he should have been the rep for those freaking boxers.

My gaze lingered on the outline of his dick through the cotton material of his underwear. As I watched, my cheeks began to heat with a mixture of embarrassment and need as I witnessed his dick grow with obvious arousal.

"That bath looks big enough for two, sweetheart. Do you care if I join you?" Wroth asked as he moved away from the door.

Unable to form coherent words, I just nodded, then shook my head, then nodded again not sure how to tell him I wanted him to take a bath with me. He chuckled as he climbed into the tub with me, boxers and all. He sat down in the water so that he was facing me and my feet were in his lap. "You're awfully quiet, Mari," he grumbled with a knowing grin.

Damn him, I loved that grin. It didn't often make an appearance and when he did grin, or even smiled, it was like a kick to my heart. I loved when he was happy. Tried my hardest to make sure he smiled and laughed at least once a day when he was home with me.

"I guess I'm just tired," I excused after finally finding my voice and clearing my throat. "I didn't sleep very well." And it was all his fault. The kiss—kisses—from the night before were still haunting me.

Wroth picked up one of my feet and started massaging, digging his thumb into my high arch in a way he knew made my eyes roll back into my head with pleasure. "I didn't sleep too great either. Some chick kissed me last night and I couldn't get the feel of her lips on me, her hands on me out of my head." He rubbed harder and I couldn't help the groan that escaped me at how good it felt. His words melted away my earlier shyness and I opened my eyes to find his dark ones glued to my face. "I can still taste you, Mari."

My tongue rubbed over my suddenly dry lips. "I can still taste you, too," I whispered.

At my confession, he made a growling sound in the back of his throat. I'd learned last night, as my hands had explored his chest under his shirt while we'd kissed for more than half an hour, that he made that sound when he liked what I was doing. That growl did disturbing things to my body. Made liquid heat gather between my legs and my nipples pebble with a need that I was scared he wasn't going to fulfil.

"I want to taste your lips again, sweetheart. I want to kiss you until your lips are raw and swollen. But I can't do that right now. Not when you are so deliciously naked under these rapidly fading bubbles. I won't be able to control myself." He released my foot, placing it carefully back on his lap. Picking up my other foot, he skimmed my arch over his massive erection, making that bud hidden between my legs, that I'd learned to rub out my orgasms for this man, throb for attention from my fingers. Or his.

With one hand he massaged my arch but the other skimmed up my calf, making my sex clench with need. Without thinking about what I was doing, I let my legs fall open, silently pleading for him to touch me. There. That growling groan escaped him again but he didn't move higher than my knee before caressing back down to my ankle then repeating the same tortured path. I squirmed, my body on fire and my clitoris pulsing with the beat of my racing heart. I wanted an orgasm so bad right then I would have begged for it.

But why should I beg for it when I could give it to myself?

More heat filled my cheeks as I met his gaze boldly, but I didn't let my embarrassment keep me from giving my body what it was screaming for. My arms had been resting on the sides of the tub, but I let them fall into the water. My left hand skimmed over my softly rounded stomach and down into the curls I kept neatly trimmed. My fingers combed through the curls, tugging lightly in a way that made my sex clench with need again. The tip of my middle finger moved over my slit and between my lips.

The first touch of my soft finger over my bud made me moan. Wroth jerked at the sound and his eyes narrowed knowingly. His next breath was sucked in almost harshly, but he didn't say a word. If anything his gaze dared me to continue. Under the bubbles and water, I added a little pressure to my middle finger and rubbed in tight little circles. I should have been more embarrassed, should have felt disgusted with myself for touching myself like this in front of him, but I wasn't and I felt oddly powerful as I continued to rub my clit until I was gasping.

Wroth's breaths were coming in heavy pants, his hands no longer massaging my foot and leg but still holding onto my ankle. Wanting to have some kind of connection to him, I lifted my free foot and rubbed it over his hard stomach, feeling his defined abs as I pushed against him a little. Another growl-like groan escaped him and his lashes lowered until I couldn't see those espresso irises any longer, but I knew that he was still watching me.

I rubbed faster, glad for the warm water so that I didn't have to lick my fingers or dip them inside myself to keep getting that little bud wet. I didn't like to penetrate myself. I didn't want anyone to ever touch me there but the man now watching me with his mouth slightly open and his chest heaving from his heavy breathing.

"Marissa..." He grabbed my foot just as I let it skim over his dick. His body shuddered so hard that it made the water ripple at that small touch of my foot on him so intimately. With both feet now in his hands, he tugged roughly, pulling me across the tub without much effort because of his strength. I loved how strong Wroth was. It made me feel delicate, more feminine when I was next to him.

I went willingly, wrapping my legs around his waist and meeting his ravenous mouth with a hunger of my own. His hands wrapped around my waist, grinding my hips against his thick erection. My soapy chest rubbed against his, my nipples pressed into his flesh to cause a new kind of ache from that bud between my legs, but only added to the pleasure-filled pain of my throbbing sex.

His thick, hard dick pressed perfectly against the lips of my sex. With my legs wide open like that, my clit was exposed and his hardness was so much better than my fingers. I rubbed my sex against him harder, harder, harder until I tossed my head back, completely broke our kiss and cried out as the strongest orgasm I'd ever felt in my life consumed me.

Wroth's curse as he found his own release was lost on me as I fell against his chest, happily exhausted. Long, thick fingers rubbed up and

*down my spine and I could hear his still erratic
heartbeat that matched my own...*

Blinking away that erotic memory, I picked
up my Voss and took a long swallow to try and
cool my suddenly heated skin. That had been
only one of the few times Wroth and I had done
something like that during those first two happy
months of the spring tour the year before. Wroth
had never tried to take things further than heavy
petting, making sure that I was always taken care
of, but only getting us both off when I begged
him to let me touch him. Remembering the way
I'd pleaded with him to let me touch him filled
me with shame.

I'd begged and begged just to get to touch
him like I craved but there had been no one
begging when I'd found him with his dick in
some groupie skank's mouth.

The pain of that memory cut me deep and I
let out a pained-filled gasp that had Bishop
reaching for my hand. "You okay, Marissa?"

Fresh tears spilled over. I tried to force a
smile for the kindness he was showing me but
was unable to pull it off. "I..." I couldn't force
words past the lump in my throat so I shrugged
and shook my head.

Strong hands suddenly landed on my
shoulders and I jerked in reaction because I
hadn't been expecting it. Linc's arms left my
shoulders and lifted me easily, as if I didn't
weigh more than a sack of feathers. "Let's go
home," he said with a sigh as he ushered a pale

and teary eyed Natalie ahead of him. "You girls never give me a dull moment, you know that?"

"Where's Rhett?" I asked, noticing it was just the three of us once we stepped outside the club.

"He'll meet us at the apartment. Pretty sure it would have been signing his death warrant if he'd been seen leaving with either of you two." Linc shifted me in his arms as a taxi pulled up in front of the club and he opened the door. Natalie climbed in first and then Linc placed me on the bench seat beside her before getting in and telling the driver where we were going.

As the taxi pulled away, I glanced out the window and saw that the crowd had only grown since Natalie and I had arrived an hour or so ago.

CHAPTER 8

MARISSA

The air was on the chilly side when I stepped out of the apartment building and into the waiting van that was ready to take me, Liam, Linc, Natalie, and Rhett to where the buses were waiting for everyone to board them. I rubbed the sleep from my eyes, not caring that I didn't have a drop of makeup on or that my hair was in a messy knot on the top of my head. I was still half asleep after having stayed up most of the night before drinking wine with Natalie and pretending like I wasn't broken inside.

It was hard work pretending. I knew from experience from a time when I had to paste a brave smile on my face and act like I wasn't tired of giving up as cancer had tried to break me. Now it was Wroth who had broken me, and I couldn't help but think it was ironic that it had been Wroth who had given me the strength to continue to fight that battle but it was now him who made me want to crawl into a ball and just give up on life.

As hard as I had tried to move on, to get over my heartbreak, I'd only been deceiving myself. An hour in the same room with the man who had caused my broken heart and I was ready to just find a vein and slice.

But I couldn't let anyone know that. I might have those thoughts going through my head, but I wasn't going to further embarrass myself by letting people know that Wroth had destroyed me so utterly.

Natalie was the last to get into the van and the driver shut the door before walking around the vehicle and climbing behind the wheel. It was only then that I took a moment to glance in the back of the van where my brother was sitting with Linc. Rhett had taken the seat in front of them, but there was already someone waiting in the seat behind Liam.

"What the fuck?" Natalie gritted out as she lifted her bottle of water and tossed it over the two seats that separated us and Zander Brockman. "You should have been at the bus an hour ago, you dumbass."

Zander didn't even flinch when the bottle hit him in the chest, just opening it and taking a thirsty swallow. By the looks of him he must have been out partying because he was still wearing the shirt and jeans he'd been wearing when I'd stopped by Liam's apartment last night. Zander had been eating pizza and playing some combat game on the Xbox.

"Found some fun downtown," was his only explanation.

Natalie glared at him for another minute before turning around in our seat. Clenching her jaw, she glared out her window as we rode through the predawn traffic of New York. Sighing, I leaned my head against my own window and closed my eyes. I was exhausted, my entire body hurting from a depression that I'd given up fighting two nights ago. I hadn't slept much since then, and the only relief I'd had was when I'd drunk an entire bottle of red wine with Natalie the night before.

The van pulled into a huge parking lot fifteen minutes later and I took my time climbing out. Seven buses were already rumbling, waiting for us. Another van pulled into the lot from the opposite side, stopping right behind ours. I didn't pay any attention to who stepped out. I knew what bus I wanted on, and I was going there before anyone else could stop me.

"Rissa," Liam called as he lifted his suitcase along with my two cases from the back of the van. "Where do you want these?"

"Give them to Rhett. He said he would take care of them for me." I'd talked to both Rhett and Linc about it the night before. Neither had a problem with me bunking with Rhett since he most likely wouldn't be on that bus the majority of the time anyway.

"You are not fucking sleeping on a bus with those motherfuckers, Rissa." Liam ignored Rhett when he stepped forward to take my bags and walked around him. My cases were heavy and the old Liam would have been unable to carry all three at once. The new Liam never failed to impress me with how far he'd come. "I don't know them, you don't know them. Wroth will go rage monster on everyone's ass and I'm not fucking starting this tour off with that shit."

The mention of Wroth's name stopped me in front of one of the buses and I turned to face my brother with a glare that made him take a step back. "I don't give a flying fuck what you want. Or if it's going to make Wroth mad. You can both go fuck yourselves because I will sleep wherever the fuck I want."

The few people standing outside the buses who had been talking suddenly went very quiet and I refused to blush when I felt their eyes on me. I didn't swear very often, and even when I did I rarely used the word 'fuck'. But if Liam was going to throw that word at me repeatedly, I was going to throw it right back.

Liam's mouth opened, then closed, only to open again. I rolled my eyes at him and turned back toward the buses, looking for the one that was for the members of Trance and Alchemy. As I passed one, Lana stuck her head out of the door. "Hey, we have more than enough room. You can come with us."

I forced a smile for her, but shook my head. "Thanks, but I don't want to intrude. I'll be fine with Rhett." I loved Lana and Drake, and Nevaeh was such a sweet little girl. But being around that happy little family would only make me hurt more because I knew I would never have that. I didn't want to admit it, but I was jealous of Lana and Drake because it was so obvious that Drake loved Lana more than life itself and I ached for that.

"Okay, sweetie. But if you change your mind, our door is always open."

The bus I was looking for was at the back of the lot and I climbed on without bothering to knock. The living room area was already full. Bishop was sitting at the table with a cup of coffee in front of him while his drummer, Carver, was eating a breakfast sandwich from McDonalds. The Trance bassist, Jasper, was sitting on the floor in front of the couch with his Beats on. Dave and Jake, the two other members of Alchemy, were standing in the kitchenette eating their breakfast while Leif and Winston, the remaining two members of Trance were in the recliners already half asleep.

When I stepped forward they all went quiet and turned their eyes on me. A few of them gave me sexy grins, but the others were all giving me frightened looks. I raised a brow at Jake who was the closest to me, wondering what had made him pale and his eyes widen as if he'd seen a ghost. "What—" I started to ask, but another voice cut off my question.

"I'm not going to play your games, Marissa." My body went white hot at the first sound of Wroth's voice, only to go ice cold at the second.

I turned to face him, not scared of him in the least—unlike most of the men on the bus. Glaring up at him like I'd done Liam earlier, I refused to be affected by the sight of Wroth in sweat pants that hung off his lean hips and a white T-shirt that had a hole in the bottom. "I'm not playing games, Wroth. Now get the fuck off my bus."

His eyes narrowed when 'fuck' came out of my mouth. "Who's been talking like that in front of you, Marissa?" Wroth didn't tolerate people cursing in front of me. Most people tried to clean up their language when I was around because they didn't want to piss him off. I couldn't have cared less how people talked, but he demanded they respected me.

Too bad *he* hadn't respected me a little more.

Someone pounded on the front door and I heard Natalie calling from outside. "We leave in two minutes."

"Guess you'd better get to your bus. See you later," I told him with a smirk as I took a seat on the couch.

"Yeah," Wroth muttered. "Guess I'd better."

If I'd been expecting him to just turn and go I was sadly mistaken. Wroth stepped around Jasper and bent toward me. My heart sped up at his nearness and the scent of his body wash as I inhaled sharply made my panties wet in an instant. "What are you..?" I let out a squeak when he lifted me as if I didn't weigh the equivalent of one and a half girls and tossed me over his shoulder like a sack of potatoes. "Wroth!" I screeched as he walked off the bus. "Damn you, put me down." I pounded my fists on his back, but he didn't even flinch as he continued to walk, easily holding onto me even when I started kicking.

His grip only tightened on my legs so that I didn't land a kick to the one place I was trying to aim for: his balls. Feeling one large hand on my thigh and the other on my ass, I quieted and remained stiff in his hold. When he paused in front of a bus I was all too familiar with, I clenched my eyes closed. "I hate you," I whispered brokenly.

After taking a few steps inside the bus, he sat me down on a recliner and straightened. I noticed that the living room was empty and was thankful for that small blessing so I didn't have to further embarrass myself in front of everyone. Wroth's eyes were shuttered, his jaw clenched hard enough that I was pretty sure he was going to break his fillings. "Hate me all you want, sweetheart. But you are going to ride this bus or stay home. And I don't mean that damn apartment here in the city. I'll send you straight back to the farm. So, your choice, Rissa. This bus or back to Tennessee. But those are your *only* choices."

"You can't make me go back to Tennessee." I stood so that he wasn't towering over me. Not that it really mattered. Wroth was so tall that he easily stood a foot taller than me. My head barely reached his shoulders. "You don't own me, and I sure as hell am not your responsibility. You can't make me do anything I don't want to do."

"You're right." His eyes darkened and he lowered his head until we were on eye level. "I can't make you do anything you don't want to do. But I can have Emmie keep you from going on tour with us. And then Liam will worry about you being in the city all alone, and we both know that you won't let him worry about you. So you will end up at the farm where he knows you will be okay."

I pushed him away, making him step back since I'd caught him off guard. "You are such a dick," I snapped. But I didn't argue with him further. He was right. If he wanted me off this tour he would make Emmie kick me off, and I wasn't going to put my brother through three months of constantly worrying about me being safe in New York. So I'd end up in Tennessee.

I didn't want to go near the farm. It was no longer my home, but a place where my broken dreams were now buried. For so long I'd dreamed of growing old on that farm, of being Wroth's wife and raising a family there.

So I would have to grit my teeth and stay on this bus. Hopefully I wouldn't give in to the pain that was slowly destroying my sanity...

CHAPTER 9

WROTH

As soon as the door shut behind Natalie, the bus pulled out into traffic behind the first five buses. I sat on the couch glaring sightlessly at one of the flat screens that had the weather channel on, broadcasting the temperature of the city we would be in by later that afternoon.

Marissa hated me.

It wasn't something I hadn't already known, but that didn't mean it didn't hurt to hear the words actually leaving her mouth. Fuck, I wished things were different. I wish I'd never tried to push her away last year. I'd known the second I'd done what I'd done that it was a mistake and that I didn't really want to be without her. In that moment I'd realized that I was losing the best thing in my world. I'd come to terms with all my self-hate and disgust. I'd forgiven myself for the things I'd done while in the marines and even come to terms with the lifestyle I'd led after the band had taken off.

But by then I'd already fucked up and there was no going back from what Marissa had seen. No fixing what I'd done to us. All I'd been able to do was let her walk away, let her have time to forgive me. She hadn't come close to doing that in the last year, and I seriously doubted she ever would. I deserved that, I knew that I did.

Didn't mean I was going to give up, though. I was going to get her back and I was going to use this tour to do it. To show her that I was sorry for pushing her away. For so many things. If she would let me, I would spend the rest of my life making up for that night.

"You guys should get some rest," Natalie said as she dropped her ever present clipboard on the kitchenette table and slid the chair beside Linc. "It's going to be nothing but rushing once we get there."

"I'm not going back there until I know Rissa has calmed down," Liam grumbled as he lifted a cup of coffee to his lips. "Pretty sure she doesn't like me right now." His eyes raged at Linc as he set his cup down. "And you—you were just going to let her ride on that fucking bus. You're supposed to be helping me watch out for my sister, not letting her do crazy shit like that."

Linc shrugged, obviously not worried about Liam's displeasure. "She would have been fine. Rhett wouldn't have let anything happen to her."

My eyes narrowed on the muscle headed personal trainer, but I remained mute as he and Liam continued to argue about the subject. Liam was right. Linc had been paid generously to be watching out for Marissa. I knew because I was the one lining his pockets with money to guarantee that she was safe. And the fucker hadn't batted an eye when she had gotten on that bus with all those motherfuckers. Instead he'd actually wanted her to be left alone so that she could ride with Rhett. With fucking Rhett.

Jesus Christ, but I hated that fucker. Hated everything about him, but especially that he and Marissa seemed close now. So close that the damn prick was actually sleeping at Marissa's apartment. And I fucking hated that I didn't know if he was sleeping with Marissa or Natalie. I couldn't have cared less if it was Natalie. Those two could fuck all they wanted for all I cared. But if Rhett was touching my girl…

I popped the knuckles of each hand, envisioning how much pleasure I would take from smashing that damn rocker's face in. Over. And over. And over.

"Dude, you need to relax," Zander mumbled from his place beside me on the couch. "You're seriously going to break your hands and then were the fuck will we be?"

Clenching my hands into fists so that I wouldn't pop my knuckles anymore, I tried to concentrate on the television by picking up the remote and turning the channel to something other than the weather channel. As long as it wasn't raining we had perfect reception on the satellite, but I couldn't find anything to hold my attention for longer than a minute.

"Wroth, if you don't fucking find a channel and leave it there *I'm* going to break your fucking hands," Natalie snapped as she got up and took the remote from me. "I'm about five seconds away from throwing your ass from this moving bus and the damn trip just started. Not exactly the best way to start the tour, asshole." She flipped through the channels until she found one of the movie channels. It was a freaking documentary on two college football teams and their rivalry.

"Let's just play a game on the PS4," I told Zander.

"Dude, you are just asking for her to beat the shit out of you," Zander snickered, but he got up and turned on the PlayStation.

Tossing me a controller, we sat back and waited for the game to load. Natalie shot us both nasty glares and walked back toward the roosts, muttering to herself. I shot Devlin a hard look. "Your chick is batshit crazy."

"Fuck, I wish she was still my chick," he muttered almost to himself. "Don't talk about her like that, man."

"True is true," Zander said with another snicker. "You fuckers all know how to pick 'em. First it was Gabriella..." Liam flipped him off. He didn't react well to the sound of Gabriella's name, and I couldn't help wondering for the hundredth time why he didn't just call her and sort out whatever the hell it was that had made him turn his back on her. Was it really because she had broken up with him right before his last stay in rehab? "...then Dallas. Now it's Nat and I think even Rissa has flipped her lid. Fuck it. Let's just go ahead and admit that all chicks are batshit crazy."

"Amen," Linc said with a grin as he took a drink of his coffee. "That's why I keep to dicks. It's less complicated that way."

Liam snorted his coffee up his nose at that and started coughing. For the first time in a long time I actually felt a grin teasing at my lips. I was relieved that Linc was gay. It meant that I didn't have to worry about him trying to get into Marissa's pants... Rhett on the other hand... Yeah, I wanted to slaughter that little fucker. Especially if he had already gotten into her pants.

Around lunch time the buses stopped and Axton climbed on board. We spent the next few hours going over our playlist for the night and rehearsing. It was our normal routine while on tour, so that we didn't have to worry about it once we got to whatever venue we were preforming at. If the noise from our rehearsal woke Marissa or Natalie, neither came out to complain about it.

I hadn't seen Marissa since she had stormed off before the bus had filled up with everyone else. I'd wanted to go back into the roosts and confront her, comfort her, but Liam had taken one look at my face and told me to give her a few days to cool off. Halfway through our set list, Natalie came out and nuked something in the microwave, completely ignoring everyone around her. Devlin's eyes locked on her the moment she walked in and didn't leave her until she walked back toward the roosts with her food.

Poor bastard.

CHAPTER 10

MARISSA

My head was killing me and the sound of the guys jamming from the front of the bus wasn't helping.

I hadn't been able to sleep. Instead I found a roost and just stared up at the bed above mine. Silently crying, hurting...trying to talk myself out of doing something stupid. It wouldn't do Liam any good if he found me in a puddle of my own blood. I had to think of Liam. He was the only one who mattered.

So I curled up into a ball and closed my eyes, letting the tears fall and the pain consume me.

"You asleep, Rissa?" I'd heard Natalie come back not long after the bus had started moving, but thankfully she hadn't tried to talk to me until right then. She'd taken the roost right above mine and I hadn't heard anything from her until now.

I wiped my damp eyes and rubbed my aching head. "Nope."

"Can I come lie down with you?" Her question was softly spoken, as if she were scared I would turn her down.

The thought of having someone hold me for just a few minutes made my chest ache. "Yeah, come on."

When the curtains of my roost were pulled back, I saw that Natalie's eyes were just as red and puffy as my own. Obviously I wasn't the only one who had been having a pity party today. I opened my arms, silently offering her the love and understanding that we both needed. Natalie climbed in, closed the curtains and then cuddled up to my side, her head resting on my shoulder.

Some of my earlier pain faded until it was almost bearable and I breathed a sigh of relief. Natalie and I lay there for nearly an hour, neither of us speaking, but we didn't sleep either. Eventually her stomach grumbled and mine wasn't any better. She offered to make us a snack and I accepted with a smile and a nod. "Be right back."

Ten minutes later she produced a frozen pizza and a bag of baked chips with two bottles of water. I sat up as much as I could and nibbled on a slice of the pizza while she opened up the chips and started crunching away. When the food was gone and our stomachs were no longer demanding attention I lay back down, listening to the band continue to rehearse and trying to tune out the sound of the guitar solos.

Natalie remained where she was but I could tell that her earlier pain was turning into a burning fury. I wished I could get that mad, and stay that mad. It would be so much better than all the pain I was feeling…

I grimaced at my thoughts, hating that I sounded like such a wimp. Suddenly I hated myself for letting a man do this to me. For giving him the power to make me hurt to the point that I had actually been considering... Yeah, that wasn't me. I was stronger than that, damn it.

Glancing at Natalie's set jaw and her angry eyes only made me even angrier. Men were such pigs. They thought they could walk all over us, cheat on us, or even make bets on whether they could sleep with us. I wanted to hurt the two men who had destroyed me and my friend. I wanted to make them pay.

"I keep thinking about that fucking bet," Natalie said, twisting the napkin in her hands until it started to tear. "How could they…*he* do that to me? I thought we had something special, but all I ended up being was some kind of immature fun for him and damn Zander."

I don't know why the idea suddenly entered my head. I wasn't a vindictive person, but the past year had seriously changed me. Hardened me. The grin that suddenly lifted my lips was evil and I didn't care. "Let's have a little immature fun of our own, Nat."

"I love you and all, Rissa, but I've never been interested in experimenting with a girl before."

For the first time in what felt like a million years I burst out laughing. I gripped my sides; I was laughing so hard it hurt to breathe. "No, no," I got out through my giggles. "I wasn't going to suggest that."

"Oh," Natalie said and grinned. "Sorry. What were you going to say?"

Wiping my eyes with the back of my hand, I sat up again and moved closer to Natalie so that no one else would hear if they happened go come back there. "I was thinking about that bet that Dev and Z made. How about we make one of our own?"

Blue-gray eyes widened and then the evil grin I'd had on my face earlier broke across her beautiful face. "You've roused my interest, my friend."

"Let's make them sweat. It's obvious that both Devlin and Wroth want us to take them back. Especially Devlin, he's like a kicked puppy when he's around you."

Natalie's grin faltered. "Wroth isn't much better, Rissa."

"Whatever, I don't care." I didn't. I. Didn't. "I don't want a man who is going to cheat on me."

"And I don't want one who treats me as nothing more than a game."

I caught her hand and gave it a reassuring squeeze. "So let's make *them* the game. I bet you that I can make Wroth beg me for another chance, seduce him and then drop him before you can do the same to Devlin."

"You want me to seduce Devlin?" Natalie whispered fiercely. "Have you lost your fucking mind? I don't want to get within touching distance, let alone let him kiss me."

I shrugged. "I didn't say it was going to be easy. They deserve some payback for breaking our hearts. It's not fair that they got to move on while we are stuck in misery. It's obvious that they want another chance, so we will let them think they can have it, let them get their hopes up, their hearts invested. And then we get one last good fuck, the closure that we both need, and drop their asses, shatter their hearts like they did ours. Don't tell me that the idea doesn't tempt you, Nat."

She bit her lip, taking her time to think over my offer. Yes, I knew that it made us little better than Devlin or Zander making their bet, but I really didn't care. I wanted my revenge, and if Natalie didn't want to participate then I'd still go through with it on my own with Wroth. I wanted to make him beg, and I wanted for him to give me what he'd denied me the first time around. I wanted him to be my first lover, and then I was going to leave him broken and bleeding as I walked away. Just as he had done to me.

Just like I still was.

"What are we betting?" Natalie finally asked. "What does the winner get?"

I hadn't really thought that far ahead. "If you win, I'll take over your job for a week and you can take a vacation."

"Holy shit that would be awesome." Natalie rubbed her hands together, apparently warming to the idea. "Okay, okay. So if you win, I will switch rooms with you."

I offered her my hand, the idea of having the larger room back at our apartment adding to the incentive to win our bet. "Deal."

"Wait, what is the time frame? How long do we get to accomplish everything?"

I shrugged. "Everything has to be accomplished by the end of the tour." That sounded like a reasonable time frame. Three months was plenty of time to torture Wroth Niall in my book.

"Okay then. Deal."

CHAPTER 11

WROTH

Natalie was spot on that we would be doing nothing but rushing once the bus stopped outside the arena where we would be preforming tonight. While Trance and Alchemy got ready to go on stage to open, OtherWorld and Demon's Wings had to do meet and greets and sign merchandise for fans. Our road crews had arrived two hours before us and were already setting things up for us, like each band's merchandise tents and our equipment.

I didn't see more than a glimpse of Marissa here and there for the rest of the day. Since OtherWorld was closing tonight—and then Demon's Wings would close at the next concert before switching back and forth for the rest of the tour—it was past midnight before I made it back to the bus. I was exhausted, grumpy, and still wired from our closing performance that had had the sold out stands shaking from the fans as they screamed our names. That never failed to get my blood pumping and now I was too wound up to relax.

When I got back to the bus it was to find Shane, Harper, Axton and Dallas waiting in the living room. They were all dressed up as if they were going out. I didn't feel like going out. All I wanted was to find my roost, see if I could talk Marissa into lying down with me so that I could finally relax and maybe I would finally get some decent sleep for once. It felt like I hadn't had a full night's sleep in a decade. I either couldn't fall asleep because thoughts of Marissa would always haunt me, or I would wake up reaching for her only to find the bed beside me empty. When that happened, I couldn't fall back to sleep no matter what I did.

Of course I knew that convincing Marissa to willingly come near me would be a miracle in and of itself. Which was made even more blindingly obvious when Marissa walked down the narrow hall dressed in club clothes with Linc. My jaw clenched so hard that my teeth began to ache when a third person appeared behind them.

Rhett Fucking Tomlinson.

"We're ready," Marissa announced with a smile as she sat down on the couch next to Dallas so that she could put her shoes on.

"Your hair smells good," Dallas said with a sigh as she leaned forward to sniff Marissa's hair. "What shampoo do you use? I want it."

I didn't hear what Marissa said because Rhett sat down on the arm of the couch beside Marissa and wrapped his arm around her shoulders. Linc joined them by lifting Dallas and sitting in her spot, carefully arranging her on his lap. Beside him, Axton grumbled something snarky that made the muscle head laugh but he didn't move.

"Hey, Wroth," Harper greeted when she spotted me standing in the doorway. "Want to come clubbing with us?"

I turned my gaze to the beautiful woman sitting beside her husband and some of the rage I was feeling at the sight of some other bastard touching my girl eased. Just a little. Harper wasn't anything like the girls I'd seen Shane Stevenson with for so many years. She was gorgeous, but it wasn't all outward packaging. She was sweet, gentle, reminding me of Marissa in so many ways that I would have given Shane a run for his money over the chick if Marissa hadn't already owned me. Harper was also broken, something that you could see in her startling violet eyes; but I admired her deeply for how brave she had been. Not many people could deal with all the things that she had to go through.

"Who's all going?" I asked, offering her a small smile.

"All of us plus Natalie, maybe Jesse. Devlin and Zander most likely. And I think Felicity is going to come with us. Emmie wants her to have some fun too." Harper stood and sat on Shane's lap, something that the Demon's Wings bassist looked more than happy to accept. "Here, you must be tired. Take my seat."

Before I could move toward the offered seat the door opened behind me. Jesse stuck his head inside. "Hey, the limo is waiting. Let's go. I want a beer."

Clubbing had not been on my mind for ways to end the evening, but there was no way in hell I was going to let Marissa go out without me. Especially if the fucker who stood to follow her off the bus was going to be with her. Just the thought of him out with Marissa made my blood boil. So with a frustrated sigh I followed Shane and Harper off the bus and then climbed into the back of a waiting limo.

Natalie, Felicity Bolton, Zander, Devlin and Jesse were already inside waiting. Felicity, a hot chick with short obviously dyed red hair and a curvy body sat between Zander and Jesse with her legs crossed in front of her. She was Emmie and Nik's nanny and from what I had heard she did a really good job at taking care of the kids. I'd also heard that Zander had tried to get in her pants once—and only once. Felicity wasn't looking for hookups or even a relationship apparently. Or so Axton had assured me when he had eventually stopped laughing his ass off long enough to tell me how convincing Felicity had been when she had told Zander to get lost.

With a knee to the balls.

The chick had grit and I respected that.

Once I was seated, there were limited spots to choose from. Shane got in behind me and Harper climbed onto his lap. Axton sat with Dallas on his lap, his hand going automatically to her still flat stomach. The way those two kept reproducing they were going to have their own rock band within a few years. Rhett and Linc got in with Linc having to sit between me and Devlin and Rhett to squeeze in between Natalie and Shane, leaving Marissa the last one to get in.

She stuck her head in and huffed. "Okay, now where is my big ass going to sit?"

"Marissa!" Dallas, Natalie, and Harper all scolded her with a glare.

"Hey, my ass makes two of any of yours. So yeah, it's big. Now where do I sit?"

Before I could open my mouth, Linc reached forward and pulled her inside. "Your sexy ass is going to sit right here." He arranged her on his lap and then buried his face in her neck, making her giggle. "Damn girl. You smell so good. If I didn't like dick so much I'd totally be all over you."

I gritted my teeth, silently repeating to myself that Linc was gay and I had nothing to worry about. There was no reason to rip his spine out through his throat. None at all.

Rhett and Natalie's snickers caught my attention, distracting me momentarily from thoughts of wanting to destroy the man who had been able to help Liam turn his life around so completely with the personal training he provided. Rhett had his arm around Natalie's shoulders, whispering something that was making them both crack up. The way those two acted around each other was a lot like the way Rhett and Marissa acted. It confused the hell out of me.

Who was he really after? Which one of them was he actually sleeping with?

Devlin grunted at the sight and turned to pound on the partition that separated the back from the driver. "Let's get the fuck going," he barked and the limo pulled out into traffic.

Traffic was still pretty backed up from all the fans going home from the concert so it took a good thirty minutes before we got to the club in downtown Chicago. When we got there we went straight to the VIP room that was on the second floor and had its own bar. Surprisingly, Emmie and Nik were already there along with a few of the members of Trance and Alchemy.

"How did you get here before us?" Jesse demanded as he took the bottle of Corona that Emmie offered him. "I thought you weren't leaving until later."

"Interesting story," Nik said as he handed me a bottle of Bud. I took a thirsty swallow as he explained how their driver had taken a detour that had gotten them to the club ten minutes ahead of us even after they had left after us.

"I'm surprised that Emmie let the driver live," Natalie commented as she took a long swallow from her glass of Sprite.

"He might be alive, but he won't be forgetting Em anytime soon. Not with that black eye she gave him," Bishop, the lead singer for Alchemy assured everyone with a hard laugh. "But I realized a valuable lesson. I'm never gonna piss her off."

"Yeah, you'll live longer that way," Nik assured the man with a grin. Wrapping his arms around his wife, he leaned back in his chair, sipping at his own beer.

For the next hour I turned my attention to drinking beer and trying not to let my eyes stray too often toward Marissa who was doing everything she possibly could to avoid me but also gain my attention all at once. She didn't drink her usual white wine, instead going straight for shots with Felicity, Rhett, Carver, Dave, and Linc. She laughed and squealed as she danced with several of Trance's band members all at once, then wrapped her arms around Rhett's waist and swayed back and forth to a slow song with her head on the rocker's shoulder.

If she wanted to make my blood boil she was doing a flawless job of it. And the madder I got, the more beer I drank. Two hours in I was feeling the effects of a few too many beers and the need to make Marissa and every fucking body else know that she belonged to me and only me.

She was out on the dance floor with a glass of something fruity in one hand and her other hand wrapped around Rhett's arm as she danced between him, Natalie and Linc. I slammed my now empty bottle of beer down onto the bar top, making Emmie—who had been standing close by—jump. But I didn't think to apologize. My mind was cloudy but focused on only one mission.

Kiss Marissa.

"Fuck, why am I the only sober one when he is suddenly shit faced?" I thought I heard Axton whine behind me.

Was I shitfaced? Maybe, but I didn't care.

As I strode toward my girl, someone stepped in front of me, but I pushed past him, not caring if I knocked the man on his ass or not. As I drew closer, Natalie and Linc stopped dancing and Natalie took a few steps back, pulling Linc with her. After a small hesitation she reached for Rhett and tugged him back with her and the muscle head. Marissa, oblivious to her friends' desertion and my approach continued to sway to the soft music with her eyes nearly closed.

My buzzed mind decided to take advantage of her like that and I wrapped my arms around her from behind. My hands folded around her waist and I lowered my head even as she stiffened in my arms. Burying my nose in her neck, I inhaled like a man deprived of oxygen would take in lungful after lungful of fresh air. Dallas had been right earlier. Marissa's shampoo did smell good. It was something different from what she had once used, but it smelled delicious and made her hair soft and shiny.

Marissa tried to turn in my arms but I tightened my hold around her waist, locking her in place against me. As if it had developed a mind of its own, my tongue snuck out and tasted the soft skin under her ear, rewarding me instantly with a shiver that she was unable to contain. Around us everyone else disappeared and I swayed to the music with her. I didn't dance, but if it meant I got to have her in my arms then I would do the fucking Macarena.

The feel of her in my arms, the taste of her skin on my tongue and her body brushing against mine as I forced her to dance with me was working havoc on my body. With the seven beers I'd consumed lowering my inhibitions, I was powerless to control the hunger that was starting to consume me. With a groan that sounded like a growl even to my own ears, I turned her around to face me.

Blue eyes stared up at me with a mixture of hurt, confusion, and anger. Her mouth, that beautiful luscious mouth, opened to say something but I fused my lips to hers and swallowed whatever she had been about to say. She stiffened in my arms even more, but I brushed my lips back and forth coaxingly until she relaxed against me and began to kiss me back. The taste of her invaded my senses, consuming me with her honey flavored essence. I wanted more, craved more. I felt her sigh more than heard it and her hands grabbed hold of the hem of my T-shirt and pulled me closer.

Everything in the room faded until there was just me and Marissa. Her nails biting into my back as she kissed me back with a passion that rivaled my own.

THE ROCEKR WHO CHERISIES ME

CHAPTER 12

MARISSA

One minute I was dancing with my friends, having a nice time even though I was tipsy and on my way to being drunk. I'd been determined to forget that Wroth was even in the room with me, and with each drink I consumed, the easier it was to pretend. When you were on your way to drunk town it was surprisingly easy to pretend.

The next minute I was in his arms, the feel of his front pressed to my back making my entire body come alive even as my heart beat my chest to death with a mixture of excitement and hurt. I'd felt the tears start to burn my throat because it felt so good to have his arms around me while he swayed to the beat of the music with me. Another thing that came easy when nearly drunk? Your emotions easily came bubbling to the surface. It wasn't so easy, however, to hide them once they did. I wasn't so sure I liked that and decided then and there that drinking so much was a bad idea. One I wasn't likely to make again anytime soon.

And then I was facing him. A million different things bubbled up in my throat to scream at him but I didn't get the chance to express one of them before his lips were on mine. I tried to remain impassive, to not respond to the heat of his mouth on me. I didn't want to want him. My body, treacherous bitch that it was, didn't give me an option before it shut down my brain and I was kissing Wroth back with a need that had been lying dormant for far too long.

Wroth tasted bitter from the beer he had been drinking, something I'd been unable to not notice as the night had gone on. He'd been drinking far more than I could ever remember him drinking in the past. I'd been concerned for him as I'd watched him drain beers five and six and when the bartender had given him beer seven I'd turned away, trying to force myself not to care that he was getting drunk.

The bitter taste of the beer, however, didn't hide the underlying deliciousness of Wroth's own particular taste. I gripped him harder, my nails sinking into his thick skin as I followed his tongue with my own and relearned the contours of his sexy mouth. I felt his rumbling groan against my aching breasts, telling me he liked my exploration.

The fact that we were in some VIP room with over fifteen other people that we knew and a few other people that we didn't wasn't a concern for me right then as I swallowed his taste over and over again. Drinking up his kisses as if I'd been lost in the desert for a year and he was the first drink of life-giving water. Between my legs my expensive panties that I'd ordered from my favorite website were growing damp from the desire that was robbing me of coherent thoughts. I wanted Wroth so badly. All thoughts of getting back at him, of making him hurt the way he had hurt me, were wiped from my mind for the moment as I took everything he was willing to offer.

When Wroth finally lifted his head, I was unable to comprehend it for a second and then I blinked my eyes open and met his espresso eyes. His pupils were dilated with desire to the point that there was no color left. His nostrils flared as if he were trying to inhale me with each breath he took. I blinked again, only just then realizing that my nails were so deep into his back I was probably drawing blood. Swiftly I dropped my hands, but didn't know what to do with them as I took a step back from him.

With distance came sanity and the desire was exchanged with anger. "Why did you do that?" I demanded, taking another step away from him.

"Because I couldn't stop myself," he responded, his voice low and almost animalistic it was so choked with desire. "I've missed the taste of you, Mari. I've missed *you*. I can't stand that you won't let me near you."

The pain that twisted his face made me hurt and I lowered my eyes so that I didn't have to see it. His confession that he missed me was like an arrow to the chest, digging deep into my heart. I'd missed him too. Probably more than he had missed me. Our short-lived relationship was like a slide show through my mind every night before I fell asleep. Of course the slide show was always followed by the big screen performance of the ending to that fleeting relationship. And it would make the pain come back with a vengeance and I'd be left curled into a fetal position as I fell asleep each night with tears drying on my face.

Thinking of the pain I had to live with on a daily basis reminded me of the payback I was going to have by the end of this tour. I should start it all right now, give in to him and let him think I was malleable, ready to start where we had left off before I'd confronted him about what I'd walked in on that horrible night...

But not yet. I wasn't ready to start letting him close again yet. I had to school myself in hardening my heart so that when the tour was over and I left Wroth with a broken, bleeding heart, I wasn't going to be wrecked all over again myself.

Raising my head, I met his gaze momentarily before hurriedly looking away, to my left where Natalie, Linc, and Rhett were still dancing but watching me closely. They all looked concerned but I knew that Rhett was the most concerned of the three. Unlike Natalie and Linc, Rhett knew that I'd been fighting bouts of depression that were so atrocious that I had to battle thoughts of suicide. I'd confessed it to him earlier and swore him to secrecy. He'd agreed, but only after begging me to come to him if I had any more thoughts like that.

"Mari-" Wroth began but I shook my head, unable to deal with him and the pleading look in those espresso eyes of his.

"No." I shook my head and took another step back. "I can't. Not yet. I just…can't."

He let out a long, pain-filled breath. "I know. I messed up bad, sweetheart. I know that. But do you think…" Wroth shook his head, a grimace contorting that face that I still foolishly loved. "Do you think that…maybe..?"

"I don't know," I told him honestly. "Just give me time."

He lifted a hand and I wasn't quick enough to step back and avoid it as he cupped my chin and stepped forward to press a kiss to my forehead. I closed my eyes tightly, savoring this gentle side of a man who was not gentle and never had been. Except with me. He'd always made me feel special, cared for. Precious. Cherished.

"I'd wait the rest of my life if it meant that you would forgive me."

The words were a low rumble that brought tears to my eyes. And then he stepped back, turned and walked out of the room. Leaving me standing there with tears pouring down my face.

I'd only been standing there a few seconds when an arm wrapped around my waist and a head leaned against my shoulder. I didn't have to look to know it was Emmie, but I was thankful for her presence. "Okay?"

I wiped my tears away with the back of my hand and shrugged. "Who knows?"

Emmie made an empathetic noise and hugged me. "It gets better, sweetie. And for what it's worth…" She lifted her head and met my eyes with a knowing light in those big green eyes of hers, "I'm pretty sure he's suffered just as much as you have. And take it from someone who knows, when your man hurts, you hurt ten times as badly."

CHAPTER 13

WROTH

I woke up with a splitting headache. It wasn't anything new to me. For the last year I'd been waking up with a hangover more often than not. It was just easier to fall asleep when my mind was so numb it had no choice but to shut down. But the only thing it really gave me was a better understanding into the mindset that Drake Stevenson had had for so many years and why he had always been seen with a bottle in his hands up until he'd met and married Lana.

It was getting old though, this pounding that felt like I had fallen asleep on top of jackhammer. The bad taste in my mouth along with the nausea rolling in my stomach weren't a plus either. How was I supposed to win Marissa back if I was sick all the time from trying to forget her long enough to grab a few hours of sleep? This man, the one I was right then with the taste of stale of beer on my tongue and my head and stomach debating which was going to be the cause of my death, was not a man Marissa would be proud of.

Groaning, I rolled over in bed and nearly fell out of the roost I'd drunkenly picked last night when I'd come back to the bus. Muttering curses that I didn't let anyone else utter within hearing distance of Marissa, I carefully climbed out of bed and took a moment to let the little men in my head stop using my brain for a trampoline and my stomach to settle a little before taking another step.

The smell of coffee was prominent in the air and I slowly made my way through the bus in search of caffeine. The bus was still moving and a glance at the watch on my wrist told me it was just after one in the afternoon. Almost everyone was still asleep from the quietness of the bus, but there were two people sitting at the table when I finally reached the front.

Linc was wide awake with Liam sitting across from him at the little kitchenette table. To say I was surprised would have been the understatement of the decade. The old Liam would have been the last man to get up, he would have been holed up in his roost with an eight ball of coke or some meth and his pipe and we would have had to wait for him to be coherent enough to start jamming so that we could get our rehearsal in before we reached whatever venue we happened to be preforming at that night.

This new Liam was up at the crack of dawn, ready to work out with Linc and get his day started right. My little cousin wasn't so little anymore. He was nearly as big as I was in the muscle department now and his once almost jaundiced eyes shone bright with a new passion for life. My surprise was replaced with pride for the man who I'd grown up with and loved like a brother.

"Dude, you need a shower," Liam complained when I dropped down beside him at the table with a huge mug of black coffee that smelled like Jesse Thornton's special concoction. "You smell like warm beer and something just as nasty."

I lifted my half closed eyes at him for a fraction of a second, any longer and my aching head would have exploded all over the table. "Welcome to one of the joys that you used to put me through, cuz."

"Go get cleaned up, Wroth."

"When I've finished that pot of coffee over there I will," I assured him as I took a long swallow of the scalding brew. When half the mug was gone, I was starting to feel a little more human and leaned back in the booth with a relieved moan.

"So is she okay?" Liam asked after a few more minutes of silence.

"She's refused to talk to me about it," Linc replied. "She never confides in me anymore, especially about him."

My eyes popped open and my heart clenched thinking they were talking about Marissa. I'd left her last night with tears falling down her cheeks and gotten trashed in some bar on the cab ride back to the buses. Had I hurt her even more than I already had without realizing it?

"Rhett said that she was crying in the bathroom for over an hour." Liam shook his head in disgust. "Devlin needs to get his head out of his ass, tell her he loves her, and put a ring on her finger before she really does decide to move on."

Relief washed over me for a moment that they had been talking about Natalie and not Marissa. But it was short lived...

"Rissa wasn't any better, man. Rhett's worried about her. When I asked what was going on, he refused to tell me, but kept repeating that we needed to keep an eye on her." Linc downed the rest of his coffee and set the empty mug on the table between us, his eyes telling me just how much he disliked me. I didn't flinch away from that hard glare. I knew that it was my fault that Marissa was in so much pain. But I was trying to fix things, damn it. If she would just let me in for five minutes I could make her love me again.

I didn't comment, however. Just finished my coffee and three more cups before going to take a shower. The coffee had helped with the little men jumping on my brain, but the shower woke the rest of my body up. I felt like a different man as I dried off and dressed in my favorite tattered jeans and an OtherWorld shirt that was at least five years old.

By the time I returned, most of the others were up and moving around. Liam was still sitting with Linc at the table and Zander was standing at the fridge with a box of cereal in one hand and a gallon of milk in the other. He was dressed in nothing more than a pair of basketball shorts and I was about to tell him to put a shirt on when I saw that Marissa was sitting on the couch with Natalie…

And sitting right between them was Rhett Fucking Tomlinson.

For fucking real? I knew for a fact that the bus hadn't stopped any since I'd gotten up so that meant the fucker had been on the bus all night. All. Fucking. Night. Had he slept with Marissa last night? Had they had sex while I was passed out? I was going to tear him limb from limb if that was the case.

"What the fuck is Tomlinson doing on here?" I blinked, because while the words were screaming through my brain they hadn't been spoken by me. Turning, I found Devlin standing right behind me, his aquamarine eyes like lasers trained on Rhett's head. "Did he sleep here?"

Of the five of us in OtherWorld, I'd always thought of Devlin as the level headed one of us all. He was the one with the teenaged kid, the one that had to make the hard decisions when it came to parenting and work. Normally he was the one who looked at things from all sides, got all points of view before he started running his mouth. Yet when it came to Natalie he wasn't level headed at all. He was easy to piss off, ready to rage and destroy anything that happened to be in the path of what he wanted.

"I slept here," Rhett confirmed when Natalie didn't look like she was going to open her mouth.

I doubted she'd even heard anything that Dev had just said the way her eyes were locked on his bare chest at the moment. He met Devlin's eyes with a boldness that was either really stupid or really gutsy. The next words out of his mouth proved to me that he was the former more than the latter. "Marissa asked me to."

Some of the tension in Devlin's body eased, but it only transferred to me. Times a billion. "You're fucking kidding me. Right?" I was talking louder than I normally would have done, making me sound more like a bear than human, but I couldn't seem to help it. I was about to scream the place down if what that little prick was saying was the truth. My eyes went straight to Marissa who was sitting calmly beside the rocker as if she wasn't tearing me apart inside. She had to know that it would kill me. "Did he sleep with you last night, Rissa?"

When she shrugged, she might as well have cut my heart out of my chest. It might have hurt less if she had. "He slept in my bed last night…" She bit her lip as if debating continuing before she shrugged again. "But sleeping was all that happened if you really must know."

"Oh, I really must know," I bellowed and before I could even realize what I was doing I was standing in front of both of them. Someone pulled Natalie up off the couch, out of danger, and Rhett was smart enough to shrink back against the couch as I leaned down and put my face in Marissa's. "You want someone to share your bed, you climb into *mine*. If I find out this

135

happens again I will kill him, Mari. Do you hear me? I. Will. Kill. Him."

"Wroth—" she began but I cut her off.

I pressed my lips hard against hers for a quick, rough kiss. "Don't," I growled when I pulled back. "Don't push me. I've killed men before, I have no problem doing it again." And this time I would enjoy it.

She didn't flinch back in fear, but her blue eyes did darken with understanding, compassion. "I know, Wroth." Her voice was gentle, as if she were talking to a wounded animal. Maybe I was. It felt like I was bleeding on the inside. Damn her and damn my love for this woman. The pain was overwhelming, making my breathing come in sharp pants.

She raised a hand and cupped the side of my face. "But that wasn't your fault. You had to kill those men or be killed yourself. If anything, I'm glad you did that. You came home, Wroth, and I don't care what you had to do to make that happen." She pushed me back and I went without giving it a second thought. I might be ready to kill the man sitting beside her but I would never physically hurt Marissa.

She stood and then her arms were wrapping around my waist. "You don't have to kill Rhett. He didn't do anything wrong. We're just friends, I swear."

Having her arms around me calmed me like nothing else ever would. *Fuck, I'd missed this.* Her assurance that she didn't blame me for having to kill men, that doing the things I'd done wasn't my fault, was almost like a healing salve to my soul and I buried my face in her neck. Her long, glorious hair hid my face and I let my guard down for a moment as I let her acceptance wash over me like a baptism of forgiveness. It was what I'd always needed, her forgiveness—hers and no one else's—for the abysmal things I'd had to do to survive. For things that I'd felt contaminated me and would eventually infect her with the dirtiness of them. Last year I'd started to forgive myself, but now it was complete and I was able to breathe just a little easier as she rubbed soothing circles on my back.

We stood there like that for a long while. I didn't want to release her, not when she was in my arms and each inhale I took was filled with her special scent. But with her that close, my body began to respond in a way it didn't respond to other chicks any more. My dick hardened and twitched against her soft stomach. Marissa gasped in surprise and I tightened my arms around her in fear that she was going to pull away.

Someone cleared their throat behind me and I reluctantly raised my head to find Linc standing there with Natalie beside him. "Before you really do go all rage monster and start killing people, maybe I should clarify something." I raised a brow at him and he opened his mouth to speak, but Natalie jumped in, cutting him off.

"Rhett and I are friends with benefits. You don't have to worry about him and Marissa, Wroth. Rhett and I are exclusive."

Linc turned to glare at her and shook his head just as Devlin punched the wall and walked back toward the roosts, turning the air blue with the curses coming out of his mouth. While what Natalie had said was a relief, I was pretty sure that she had just lied by the look on Linc's face.

"Are you trying to get him killed?" Linc snapped when the sliding door to the roosts slammed shut so hard that the bus actually rocked. From the front of the bus the driver slowed down.

"I can take care of myself, Linc," Rhett assured him.

"You really don't know what you're getting yourself into with Dev, man," Zander commented from the kitchenette. "I still have trouble breathing at times from the last fight we got into."

Liam made an agreeing sound but didn't speak as he watched everyone around him as if we were stars in some soap opera he was interested in. Knowing him and his twisted sense of humor at times, we probably were.

Linc turned the glare on the man still sitting on the couch. Rhett didn't look particularly worried about how pissed Devlin now was. It only strengthened my conviction that the rocker was stupid. I truly was like a rage monster when I got pissed, but that meant that I was quick to take action and when it was over I was fine—for the most part. Devlin? He was like a hurricane. He started out by letting his anger simmer, until it gained steam, powering him forward and he was soon out of control. He would destroy everything in his path when he reached the peak of his wrath and there would be no stopping him.

Which would leave Rhett Tomlinson in a body bag, along with anyone else who stepped in Devlin's way.

"Look," Linc met my gaze head on, ignoring Rhett and Natalie now, "you have nothing to worry about because Rhett is with me. Not Natalie and definitely not Marissa. He might act like he's a lady killer, but that's just his beard. He likes dick." His lips lifted in a conceited grin. "Particularly my dick." Rhett snorted, but didn't deny it. "Maybe you should assure the beast now tearing the place down, before we wreck."

If the bus shook when Devlin had slammed the door a few minutes ago it was nothing compared to what he was doing back there now. I heard the loud thuds as he continued to beat the walls with his fists and clenched my jaw as the bus swerved dangerously. Sighing, I stepped back from Marissa who clung for just a moment before releasing me, and led the way back to the roosts. Liam flanked me, with Zander bringing up the rear.

I had to force the door open because Devlin had warped it when he'd slammed it shut. Or maybe it was the dozen or so indentions of his fist in the door? Either way I had to use some serious muscle to get the door open. The sight I saw when I was finally able to step inside twisted my gut. Mattresses had been pulled out of roosts. Covers, sheets, pillows and even a stuffed animal were tossed around the sleeping area. There were holes in the walls and even a dent in the ceiling.

And all of that destruction had taken less than three or four minutes and he was still throwing things.

The bus started to slow more and then pulled off onto the side of the road. I knew what was coming. Knew that we had about sixty seconds before the fires of hell arrived and engulfed us with her rage. Emmie was going to bust balls as soon as she set foot on board this bus and there was nothing anyone could do to stop it.

"Do we have to stop him?" Zander asked, staring at the carnage in front of us. "The way this place looks and from the way he keeps throwing punches at the walls, I'm pretty sure that someone is gonna end up with a bloody nose and a black eye or two. And if Emmie goes in there and deals with him someone isn't walking out alive. My money's on the hot chick."

So was mine.

The space we were standing in was narrow but Natalie suddenly appeared and pushed past us. When she was inside the sleeping area, she pushed me back and shut the door in my face. I blinked, not sure I'd just seen that little chick shut something so easily that had taken most of my strength to get open.

From the front of the bus I could hear Emmie already demanding to know what was going on and I shared a glance between the two bassists standing behind me. Did we go out there and deal with her or hide out right here? It might sound cowardly, but I'd rather face an army of enemy soldiers single handedly than one itty bitty redhead with big green eyes.

CHAPTER 14

MARISSA

The sleeping area was a disaster, but after I helped Natalie put the beds back together all that was left were a bunch of dents and a few holes in the walls. I don't know how Natalie had calmed Devlin down, but things had gotten very quiet back here not long after she had locked herself in with him. She'd either knocked him out or they'd had sex.

From the smug look on Devlin's face when he'd walked out twenty minutes later, sex had definitely been the answer. By then I'd convinced Emmie that everything was okay and that she could go back to her own bus and we'd gotten back on the road. She'd given in because even the smallest delay would throw off tonight's concert—and the possibility of Nik finding out what was going on aboard our bus would only get back to Drake and Shane and then there would be two homicidal rockers on the loose with two other rockers ready to back up their band brothers. Emmie didn't like delays or having to make fans, who'd paid good money to see the bands she represented, have to wait even a few minutes longer than they had to. And she especially didn't like having to bail her Demons out of jail, which had happened far too often with at least one of them. Jesse Thornton hadn't always been the responsible man Layla had made him.

When we had pulled over, Axton had climbed on board and now the guys were all practicing in the living room. I lay down on my bed and listened to Axton's voice and let it soothe me. I'd always liked Axton, but I liked him even more now. He was a different man with Dallas, a better man. He didn't hide his feelings anymore, let people see what he was really thinking—mostly. The last tour he'd made sure that he and Dallas had their own bus so that she could relax while in her second trimester of pregnancy with Cannon. This tour they had their adopted daughter with them, Kenzie, who was helping out Emmie's nannie by taking care of a few of the children when the parents were busy, so there were three of us who could help watch the kids during concerts.

Kenzie was a really sweet girl. She would be turning nineteen in a few weeks, but she still looked younger. Years in an orphanage, not getting enough to eat, had left the girl on the small side and no matter how much food you set in front of her she only ate smaller portions because it was so ingrained in her to do so.

Kenzie had just finished her freshmen year at Knoxville's University of Tennessee, where she was studying to be a special education teacher. Dallas had told me that Kenzie worked at a nursing home that was specifically for Down syndrome patients who had basically been abandoned by their families. Apparently the pay was little to nothing, but Kenzie was happy working there and that was all that mattered to Dallas and Axton.

From the front of the bus, a guitar solo started and I closed my eyes. Wroth's pain earlier, seeing it shining from his eyes was like a beacon drawing me in. I'd been helpless to not comfort him. Maybe I'd been the only one to notice, but his voice had cracked just a little when he had said he'd killed men before. I knew he'd had to do some horrible things while in Afghanistan, knew that that time still haunted him. When I'd still lived at the farm with him, I'd been woken up countless times to the sounds of his nightmares. I knew better than to go to him though. The one and only time I'd gone to check on him, when I was seventeen, I'd ended up with my first and only black eye from his thrashing arms. When he'd woken up and seen what he'd done, he'd made me promise to never come back during one of his nightmares. I'd promised, but there had been times when it had taken everything inside of me to keep it.

I would never hold anything he had to do to survive against him; if anything, I was grateful he'd done those things. He'd been serving his country, making our country a safer place, but it had also brought him back to me. Sure I'd just been a kid at the time, but I'd loved him even then.

I still loved him.

Hence the problem I was facing with the bet I'd made with Natalie. I'd never make another one while angry again, that was for sure. I wanted to let Wroth back in, but did I really want to walk away when it came time to make him bleed? I wasn't sure...

I must have drifted off, because a noise—or lack of noise woke me. Sighing, I opened my eyes and met the espresso gaze of the man who haunted my dreams. Gasping in surprise, I started to pull away, but his hands tightened on my waist and kept me trapped against his side. His head lowered quickly and captured my lips in a kiss that stole my breath along with my common sense.

He tasted like the coffee I'd become so addicted to lately and that made me greedy for more. My hands climbed up his chest, over the hard muscles of his neck and into his short hair, pulling his head down harder. My tongue dueled with his for entrance inside his hot mouth where I devoured the taste of coffee and something far richer. My taste buds exploded while my heart was beating against my chest as if it were trying to claw its way out of me and into him.

That groan that was more growl escaped him and his right hand drifted down my left side before cupping my rear hard enough to leave bruises, but I didn't care. I would savor the soreness later, I silently promised myself as I continued to kiss him like my life depended on it. Wroth's hand drifted lower on my hip, skimming over the seam of my rear through the yoga pants I was wearing, and then lower. Without thinking, I instinctively spread my legs a little and he dipped his fingers between them, cupping my sex.

My panties, already wet from our kiss, became drenched instantly and he made another growling sound in approval. Wroth thrust his hips forward, fitting his hardness against my sweet spot through his boxers and the rough material of his jeans and my thin layers of yoga pants and cotton panties. I couldn't continue to kiss him while he was doing that or I would end up passing out from lack of oxygen to my poor brain. I pulled away from his lips, and his head followed but not to kiss my mouth. Instead he buried his face in my neck and started nibbling, sucking, tasting me as if I were his favorite flavor of candy.

His teeth sunk into the tender spot where my shoulder met my neck and I was helpless to keep in a moan that was a mixture of pain and pleasure. More pleasure than pain, though. Much, much more pleasure. "Wroth!" I gasped his name as he withdrew his teeth only to sink them in again before pulling the flesh into his mouth and sucking. My eyes rolled back into my head and my nails sunk into his back as I held on through the almost orgasmic feeling of him sucking on my flesh like that.

"You're mine, Mari," he growled against my ear when he finally released my skin.

I closed my eyes, savoring those words and at the same time fearing them. I wanted to be his, but what if he broke my heart again? How could I have a relationship with him when I'd be constantly terrified that he was cheating on me?

Swallowing around the lump that suddenly filled my throat at the memory of the last time he'd done just that, I found the strength to open my eyes and met his desire-glazed eyes. "I am yours, Wroth. I probably always will be. But are you mine? Were you ever?" He opened his mouth but I didn't give him the chance to speak before I was pushing at his chest. My body was screaming at me to let him stay, at least until it was satisfied, but I ignored it. "Until I know that you are mine and only mine, I can't do this with you."

His eyes darkened with pain, but he left my bed without a fight. When he stood up he bent back down and leaned into my roost to brush a kiss over my forehead. "I'll prove that I'm yours, sweetheart. That you always have been and always will be. If that's what you need, then I'll give it to you, and keep giving it to you for as long as you'll let me."

CHAPTER 15

WROTH

When I left the bus it was to more than fifteen thousand screaming fans chanting our name. It was exhilarating but it didn't hold my attention for longer than half an hour. My mind and body were still on the bus, in Marissa's bed with her curled around me and my mouth tasting her flesh. I was still hard as a rock, something that hadn't changed even a little since I'd climbed into her bed while she'd been sleeping.

I'd been unable to resist the sight of her curled up on her side with her hand tucked under her cheek like some fairytale angel. All I'd meant to do was lie down and hold her for a few minutes, but once I'd had her in my arms, and then seen those sleep-filled blue eyes, the temptation to kiss those luscious lips had been too hard to fight and before I knew it things had gotten out of control.

Marissa pushing me away had not been the best feeling in the world, but in a way I was glad she had. Now I knew what was keeping us apart—her fear that I would cheat again. I could have told her then and there that that wasn't ever going to happen again. I could have explained about the last time it had happened and told her that what she had seen wasn't really what she thought—at least not as bad as she thought it was. In the end I hadn't because they were just words and Marissa didn't need the words. She needed action and proof and I was going to give it to her.

Walking back to the buses after our set, I passed two of Trance's members and nodded at them in greeting. The band had opened for us, getting the fans going with their kickass performance tonight, and I wondered briefly if they knew their lead singer was gay and sleeping with Liam's personal trainer. When Linc had confessed that it was him sleeping with Rhett Tomlinson and not Marissa—or even Natalie for that matter—I'd been too relieved finding out that he wasn't trying to get into my girl's panties to actually realize what that meant. It didn't bother me that the dude was gay, not even a little. Seriously, how many gay rockers or rockers that were at least bisexual do you think there have been in the history of rock? I knew plenty and there had been just as many over the decades upon decades of rock-n-roll.

All I wanted to do was get back to the bus and hoped that Marissa would be back. Since most of the Demon's Wings guys were back at their own buses with their kids, she wouldn't be needed. I had to pass Shane and Harper's bus to get to OtherWorld's and as I passed I heard a snarling like growl from inside the dimly lit bus. I knew that Harper had brought her German Shepard, Ranger, and figured it was just the dog growling at people as they passed the bus. But as I drifted closer to let a few of the roadies pass I heard it let out a whimper so pitiful my stomach turned. Instinct told me the dog was in trouble, and I'd passed both Harper and Shane eating pizza with Shane's youngest sister, Jenna, along with Harris who was staying on Jesse's bus, as well as Lucy not five minutes ago.

Without stopping to think about what I might be walking into, I opened the door to Shane's bus and stepped inside, noting briefly that the door looked like it had been popped open with a crowbar. Like the rest of us, our buses stayed locked up because fans went a little crazy at times and tried to sneak into our beds. In the living area I discovered that the place had been turned upside down. The flat screen was shattered and lying on the floor. The couch looked like someone had taken a large knife to it. The fridge in the small kitchenette was open and all the contents spilled on the floor.

I heard the whimper again and rushed through the bus. The bathroom door was open, showing me that the shower door was shattered. The mirror had something red written on it but I didn't pause long enough to read it. I hurried toward the whimpering sounds that were getting worse, more pitiful. The sliding door to the bedroom was slightly ajar. I pushed it back and stepped inside to find a scene that turned my stomach even after seeing the terrors of war torn cities and blown up bodies.

The bed was in shambles with the covers spread across the room. Pillows were ripped open, the mattress seemed to have had the same knife the couch had been cut with taken to it. And there, sticking his head out from under the closet was the German Shepard, lying in a pool of blood and cut open by the same knife. A knife that wasn't even close to a knife but a fucking machete because it was lying on the floor just inches from the dog.

I bent to examine him. He still had a little fight left in him because he growled a little when I touched his snout, but when I put a hand to the slices on his belly he whimpered again. His tongue stuck out of his mouth and he was panting hard. I wasn't sure how deep Ranger's wounds were but I knew that if he didn't get help soon he wasn't going to make it. I grabbed one of the blankets off the floor and wrapped it around the injured dog, carefully lifted him and ran.

I'd barely taken two steps off the bus when Shane was standing in front of me. "What the fuck..? Ranger!" His eyes darkened. "Wroth, what..?"

"I heard him as I was passing your bus. The place is a mess, man. And your dog is in bad shape. We gotta get him some help," I told him as I continued to run.

Shane followed. He pulled out his phone as he ran beside me toward the closest exit. "Em? Something's happened. Ranger..." His voice broke and he started again. "I'm with Wroth. I see one of the EMTs. We're gonna get him to an emergency vet. Find out what the hell happened on my bus and make sure Harper..." Again his voice broke, worse this time and he cleared his throat before continuing. "Just keep her safe, Em."

I had seen the EMT just as soon as Shane had and I rushed toward the man sitting on the back bumper of his ambulance. I didn't know how much help a paramedic could be to a dog, but he could at least push me in the right direction since he was a local. When he saw what I held, his eyes widened but he didn't hesitate to take the bleeding dog from me and stepped inside the ambulance. I followed him in with Shane pushing me forward until there was no more room so that he could get inside. The EMT unwrapped Ranger and started checking him over, listening to his belly and lungs before yelling at his partner in the front seat to get them to the E-Vet.

The EMT surprised me further when he put an IV into the dog's leg. Ranger was worse than I had first thought because he didn't protest when the needle went in. Shane dropped down on his knees beside the stretcher and started petting the dog's nose, whispering soothingly to the dog almost as if it was more a child than a pet. From the way I'd seen Harper treat the dog, I knew that

that was exactly what he was to her and if the dog died then she would be devastated. From the way Shane was acting, he would be too.

It took less than five minutes to reach the E-Vet because as soon as we ran into traffic, the driver hit his siren and the gas. The veterinarian's clinic was bigger than I had expected, looking more like a small hospital than a vet's office. The doors to the ambulance opened and a vet in green scrubs and his tech were waiting to take the dog. I'd heard the driver talking earlier and he must have been speaking to the staff. They placed him on a gurney and wheeled him inside. The vet started asking questions about the dog's history which Shane was able to answer and then the vet asked what happened.

"Someone sliced him up with a machete. They destroyed Shane's bus and Ranger must have tried to scare the person off," I told the vet as we all stepped into what looked like an operating room.

"Okay. I'm going to have to do some x-rays and shave him. I don't know how much damage has been done, so I'm going to have to open him up to make sure nothing vital was damaged, but he's lost a lot of blood and losing more by the second." The vet nodded toward the door. "Wait in the waiting room, guys. I'll come get you as soon as I know anything."

I nodded and started to leave but Shane just stood there, his eyes damp with tears as he stared down at his wife's dog. Grimacing, I slung my arm around my friend's shoulders and urged him out of the OR and into the waiting room. The room was empty so I pushed Shane into the closest chair and took a seat next to him.

Shane lowered his head and let his tears fall. He had always been the type of man who didn't care to show his emotions and I respected him for that. I had never been one to openly show my own emotions so I almost envied him. After a few minutes I noticed that his phone was blowing up with texts and incoming calls. Exhaling noisily, I took the thing from his slackened hand and lifted it to my ear. "Yeah?"

"Wroth?" It was Emmie and she didn't sound happy. "Is Shane okay?"

"The vet doesn't know if the dog is gonna make it or not, Emmie. Did you find out anything about who trashed their bus?"

"Peterson called in the locals and he is going over the bus with them, but it's looking like some crazy fan did it. From the message on the mirror in the bathroom—which the crazy bitch wrote in what looks like the dog's blood—I'm pretty sure that is exactly what it is. Harper was the intended victim." Emmie's voice was ice cold and full of venom. Someone had dared to mess with her family. Whoever had done this better hope they never got caught because Emmie Armstrong's wrath was not something they wanted to ever have to deal with. I almost pitied the poor fucker when they got caught. Almost. "I'm going to add some extra security and find another personal bodyguard for Harper. She might only want Peterson, but she needs at least one extra guard."

"How is she?"

"Pissed off. I haven't told her how bad Ranger is yet, though. Just that he was hurt." She blew out a frustrated breath. "She's not going to take it well if the dog dies, Wroth."

"Yeah, I figured that out by now." I glanced down at Shane who had his hands folded together as if he were praying. I'd never seen Shane Stevenson pray in all the years I'd known him. Poor bastard. "Shane isn't looking so great, Em. Maybe you should send Nik or one of the other Demons over. Someone. I'm not exactly a comforting kind of man."

"You'll do fine, Wroth. Right now I'm glad it's you. If some lunatic is on the loose, then he isn't any safer than Harper is. With your training, you're the best one to be with him right now. Watch his back." Her voice shook slightly and I realized that she was probably fighting her own tears.

I promised her I would and then ended the call soon afterwards when someone tried to get Emmie's attention. For the next half hour I sat beside Shane, watching out for him while he just sat there with his head bowed, silently praying for the life of a pet that was like his child.

The entrance door slid open and I raised my head, expecting to see some pet and its owner coming through the door. When I saw Marissa walking in, I nearly stopped breathing. She looked frazzled and worried, but no less beautiful. Her eyes met mine almost immediately and she offered me a small, sad smile as she came to sit beside me without saying a word. I sat back and wrapped my arm around her shoulders, but neither of us spoke as we waited with our friend.

When the door to the OR opened more than an hour later, it was the tech and she had a small smile on her face as she stepped forward. Her green scrub's top was damp with sweat, her hair in disarray, but the smile gave me hope.

I nudged Shane and his head snapped up. When he stood, I followed with Marissa close behind. "How is he?" Shane demanded, his voice hoarse with tears.

"The doctor is just finishing up his stitches. The blade did go deep, but thankfully nothing vital was hit. He's going to be a very sore puppy for a while, but he's going to be fine. Doc will be out in a few minutes to talk to you." She smiled, reached out and gave Shane's hand a reassuring squeeze, nodded at me and Marissa and then returned to the room she'd just come out of.

As soon as the door closed behind her, Shane lost it. He started sobbing with relief and I couldn't not hug the man. His arms wrapped around me in a vise-like hold and I awkwardly patted him on the back for a long, long time before the Demon's Wings bassist was able to get his emotions together enough to let me go. He finally pulled himself together enough to sit back down and Marissa sat on the other side of him.

"I was scared I was going to have to go back to Harper and tell her that her dog was gone," he muttered to himself.

"I'm so glad he's going to be okay," Marissa told him and his head snapped up again as if he was just then realizing that she was there.

"How is she?" Blue-gray eyes looked wild. "Is she okay?"

Marissa smiled. "Yeah, she's fine. Angry, but okay. She's asked me to tell you she loves you and she was glad you were with Ranger since she couldn't be."

Shane stood again, patting his jeans for his phone. I pulled it out of my back pocket and handed it to him since I hadn't given it back after Emmie had called. He took it and walked across the room before putting the phone to his ear. "Beautiful?" His voice cracked, it was so full of emotions that I turned away from the sight of him. It was more than obvious that Shane loved his wife more than anything on the planet. "Are you okay?" There was a pause before he cleared his throat and spoke again. "The vet said that Ranger is going to be okay. He will be out to talk to me in a minute and give me details."

While Shane talked to his wife, I sat down beside Marissa and wrapped my arm around her once again. She leaned into me, offering me the comfort I hadn't known I needed until right at that moment. "How are you?" she asked after a moment.

"I'm good. Now." I brushed a kiss across her forehead. "Thanks for coming over to stay with me."

"When Emmie said you were over here alone with him, I offered to come help. I figured you would be out of your element, especially with Shane. But you were really good with him just now." A small smile tilted her lips and she shook her head. "That was the most awkward hug I've ever witnessed, but it was also the most endearing."

I lowered my head and kissed her cheek, needing to feel some kind of connection to her without pushing her. When she shivered, my body hardened instantaneously, but I just pulled her closer and she rested her head on my chest until the vet came out to talk to Shane ten minutes later.

Ranger would have to stay overnight but would be able to travel by the next afternoon. We didn't have a concert for two days so that wasn't going to be a problem. But Shane didn't look like he cared about the next concert and I understood that. Not just because of the poor dog, but because he had so much shit to deal with.

His wife was the target of angry female fans, something she'd been from the day the story about their engagement had hit social media. Shane Stevenson's days of living it up with any female who looked twice at him were officially over that day. Apparently the two years that he and Harper had lived together hadn't counted, but as soon as they had announced they were getting hitched things had gone batshit crazy.

Now, it wasn't just the threat of those crazies doing something to hurt Harper. It was an actuality. Someone had crossed that fine line from theory to action and Harper's safety was at stake. By the time we got back to the buses, Shane was muttering about quitting Demon's Wings to protect his girl.

I didn't comment on it, because if it had been me and Marissa's safety was the one on the line, I'd be thinking the same things. I'd walk away from OtherWorld without a backwards glance to protect her.

CHAPTER 16

MARISSA

S hane and Harper's bus needed some repairs as well as having some essentials replaced, so they moved onto Drake and Lana's bus with a very sore Ranger and Jenna, who was spending the summer with them, the next evening and we headed out for the next city. The driver and two roadies would take care of everything and then meet up with us in the next city since everything would take longer than expected to fix.

Harper had convinced Shane not to quit, because no matter what he did he was always going to be Shane Stevenson. Which meant that women were always going to hate her. She wasn't going to let him give up something that was such a big part of who he was just because some psycho had tried to scare them.

Things on the OtherWorld bus were less strained the next few days. With Linc outing his relationship with Rhett, the men were all a little nicer around the Trance lead singer. If Linc hadn't admitted to being with the rocker I never would have said a word. Rhett was my friend, possibly my best friend, and I would never spill his secrets.

To my surprise, Wroth even sat down and had a beer with him one night after a concert. I'd heard them talking and Wroth had actually been laughing as I'd passed the Trance/Alchemy bus. I wasn't sure how to take that, since only a few days before, Wroth had been threatening to murder the man.

Devlin was particularly more good natured in the days that followed. Natalie was moving forward quickly with our bet, while I was taking my time. I was trying to ease back into the old relationship Wroth and I had had before letting things progress toward the revenge that I was still unsure if I wanted or not.

Wroth wasn't making my indecision any easier with the way he'd been acting lately. He was more laid back now, less strained. He laughed more than I'd ever heard him laugh before and spoke often, joining in on conversations he wouldn't have normally participated in. He was sweeter, more affectionate too, finding excuses to touch me in small, intimate ways that made me feel special and desired without feeling like he was trying to push or rush me. Little things like pushing my hair out of my eyes, or simply holding my hand while we all watched something on TV one afternoon.

Even when we had been in a relationship the year before, he'd never been one for public displays of affection, not even ones that were that small. Wroth was too private, too reserved for that kind of thing. So what was different now? What had changed with him?

Could all his rigidness have been because of his time in the marines? Had it closed him off that much?

I didn't know, but I had to admit that I liked this new side of Wroth. He was more approachable. The only real problem I had with it was that it was so easy to fall deeper for the man. I didn't want to love him more than I already did. It was so consuming as it was, any more and I knew I wouldn't walk away from him breaking my heart with my sanity intact a second time.

Today was an off day. There would be no traveling until the next morning, no concerts—no craziness. All the parents were taking their kids out to explore the local sights and I got a day of relaxing. There was only one thing I wanted to do, so I popped a bag of popcorn and fixed myself a big glass of iced tea before sitting down to watch my favorite movie of all time.

The tornado was just picking up Dorothy's house when I heard him moving around in the back of the bus. Most of everyone else had already left to do their own thing for the day, but Wroth had still been asleep. I'd debated whether or not to stick around in case he got up before anyone else came back, but had vetoed that idea almost as soon as it had entered my mind. I didn't want to avoid him. I wanted more time with him to soak up this new, softer side of him. As for the bet, I would play that by ear. It wasn't like I would be losing anything if I didn't win the bet with Natalie. Working her job for a week while she went on vacation wasn't going to be so bad. *If* I didn't win.

Wroth was still blinking sleep out of his eyes when he entered the living room. When he saw me sitting on the couch, his eyes brightened and he was smiling when he sat down beside me, scooping up a giant handful of my popcorn. "Morning, sweetheart."

"Morning," I murmured, cuddling against him just a little.

Espresso eyes went to the flat screen and he shook his head when he instantly realized what I was watching. "Really? Didn't we just watch this last night?"

"We didn't. But I watched it with Mia and the twins." I took a sip of my tea, remembering how much the three kids had enjoyed watching *The Wizard of Oz* with me. "Luca likes the Tin Man, but especially likes the flying monkeys. Lyric was more into the Lion. And Mia wants her parents to buy her a dog that is just like Toto."

He chuckled. "Sounds like that little dude. I don't know how Jesse and Layla keep up with him and his brother."

I didn't either. I'd barely been able to keep up with them the night before and I'd had Kenzie's help. Felicity had taken Neveah, Cannon, and Jagger to a different bus since they had been ready for bed. By the time Jesse and Layla had shown up to take their twins, I'd been ready for my own bed and had fallen asleep almost instantly.

"When this goes off let's watch *The Great and Powerful Oz*," Wroth suggested, digging his hand into my bowl of popcorn again.

My eyes widened in surprise. "Really?" I knew my voice broadcasted my skepticism but I couldn't help it. Wroth hated James Franco movies. That he not only wanted to watch one, but had gone so far as to actually suggest it surprised me.

"Really. Franco isn't as hard to stomach in that movie as he is in his others. And I like watching Mila Kunis turn into the ugly green witch." Another handful of popcorn was crammed into his mouth stopping any further conversation for the moment and I shrugged.

For the next four hours we watched both movies and I was content for what felt like the first time in a lifetime. Wroth sat beside me the entire time, alternating between watching the movies and watching me. One strong arm wrapped around my shoulders as I hid my face and cried—like I always did—as Dorothy said goodbye to the Scarecrow.

It felt like old times, and for a little while I could pretend that nothing had changed between us.

When *The Great and Powerful Oz* went off, Wroth stood and pulled me to my feet. "Let's go out." He didn't give me time to protest before he was linking our fingers together and leading me off the bus.

It was a nice day out, not terribly hot and the sun was shining down on us. We walked through the parking lot where all seven of the buses were parked in and hailed a cab not far from the gates. For over an hour we just rode around, talking and laughing in a way we'd never done before. The driver kept shooting us glances in his rearview mirror, smiling from time to time, but never interrupting us. Eventually Wroth had the driver drop us off at a small little Italian restaurant. I hadn't had more than the two bowls of popcorn that we had shared during our movies so I was starving by the time we were seated.

"This is nice," Wroth said, taking a sip of the red wine he had ordered to go with our pasta. Espresso eyes darkened to nearly onyx, his face twisting in pain. "I've missed you, Mari. Nothing feels right when you aren't around. The farm doesn't even feel like home anymore."

My teeth sank into my bottom lip, his words washing over me like a trembling caress. "I've missed you, too," I confessed in a voice that was practically a whisper.

"If I explained about that chick, if I told you that what you had seen wasn't as bad as you think, would you listen, sweetheart?" His eyes were almost pleading as he watched me closely.

"Maybe. I don't know. But not now. I..." I blew out a long, tear-filled breath and shook my head. "I can't yet, Wroth."

His strong jaw clenched. "Okay, but one day soon we need to talk about it. I want us to start over, to put the past behind us and build a future together." He reached across the table and grasped both my hands, linking our fingers together as he leaned forward. His naturally rough voice was full of husky gravel when he spoke again. "You are the most important person in my life, Marissa. No one else, nothing else matters to me but you. I want you to be happy, but I greedily want you to be happy with me."

Tears burned my eyes and I blinked rapidly to keep them at bay, but one wayward drop landed on my cheek. If he had said those words to me a year ago I would have fallen into his arms and given him everything. The only thing holding me back right at that moment was one small memory. A memory that had haunted me every night since it had happened...

***

I wasn't sure why, but I thought Wroth might have been avoiding me. He'd been more busy than usual the last few days and it felt like we barely had any time to ourselves. It wasn't anything unusual for him though. When he was stressed he always pulled away from people, avoiding them until he could get his emotions in check better. Over the last two months we had gotten incredibly close, more so than we had ever been. I knew that his feelings for me were growing stronger and that that was why he was pulling away right now.

That didn't mean it didn't hurt, but I had waited this long for him to confess he loved me. I could wait a little longer and even give him the space he obviously needed.

Tonight's concert was over and the guys were all seated at their own tables backstage, doing one of their rare meet and greets. The majority of the band hated these things, feeling more like a piece of meat for the fans to gnaw on rather than someone they respected. Zander and Devlin were probably the exception to the rule though. They both enjoyed meeting all the fans, proof of which was in Devlin's eyes as he talked animatedly with some guy. Even Zander seemed happy chatting with the husband and wife duo that were standing in front of his table laughing together while Zander signed the wife's back so that she could have it inked in later that night.

Liam looked bored, however, as he signed a poster and a T-shirt for the very busty chick in front of him. It was more than obvious to me that my brother was missing Gabriella, but I couldn't for the life of me figure out why he wouldn't just call her and make up with her. She'd been by his side throughout his time in a coma, only leaving when he woke up and screamed at her to get out. I didn't have anything against Gabriella, she had always been kind to me after all. I even understood why she had ended things with Liam last October. He had needed to get his act together, an act that had put her nephew in danger without her even knowing it.

Axton, who had been looking like he was going to fall asleep any minute suddenly looked more alert as he chatted with a smaller girl standing in front of him. After a few minutes he glanced over at where I was sitting with Dallas. Dallas raised a brow at her boyfriend, a silent communication passing between them before she stood and walked over to them. I didn't watch to see what happened at Axton's table next because my gaze was suddenly drawn to Wroth's table right beside of Axton's.

I'd seen the girl with the very impressive chest when she had first stopped at Axton's table. She was dressed much like the other women that I'd seen pass from table to table for the last few hours. Tight jeans, barely there shirt without a bra—not that she needed one. Her boobs had been bought and paid for and from the size and perfect shape of them, they had cost a pretty penny. At the moment those big beauties were bouncing inches from Wroth's face.

Jealousy suddenly made my stomach churn and my heart hurt. When Wroth's eyes darkened with what looked like interest, I turned away, unable to watch as he signed her breasts.

After that I avoided looking at Wroth's table. When Dallas came back to sit with me, she had the younger girl that Axton had introduced her to. I focused all my attention on Kenzie, liking the girl instantly. She was sweet, intelligent, and very excited to have gotten to meet all the members of OtherWorld.

It wasn't long afterwards that the meet and greet was over, and I quickly made my excuses to go back to the hotel. I didn't want to have to deal with anything else tonight and planned on going straight to bed once I got back.

"You wanna come with us?" Axton offered. "Wroth said he had to make sure his Fenders were stored safely. Knowing him and his love for his guitars, he might be a little while."

I forced a laugh and shook my head. "No thanks. I'm going to head back to the hotel and order some room service. I have a craving for pancakes and sausage." It was a lie of course, because after seeing Wroth and Miss Bouncy Boobs, I'd been fighting nausea ever since. I said my goodbyes and headed out to hail a cab.

It was only as the driver was stopping in front of me that I realized that Wroth had our suite key since he'd picked up both when we left for the venue that evening. It was late and I didn't want to have to deal with the moody receptionist that had been on duty when we left by asking for a new key. With a muttered curse, I waved the driver on and went in search of Wroth.

Axton said Wroth wanted to check on his Fenders so I knew exactly where to find him. The roadies always knew to take extra care of Wroth's guitars and always kept them locked up on their bus. By now most of the roadies were out grabbing something to eat or at some club downtown, but I knew where their bus was.

As I neared it, I heard a curse, realizing it was Wroth just as I walked around the side of the bus. *At first I thought maybe he had cursed because something had happened to one of his precious Fenders; he loved those things more than anything in the world. But when I saw what was really going on, I froze. Pain poured over me like a bucket of ice as I took in Miss Bouncy Boobs from earlier. She was on her knees in front of Wroth who was leaning against the side of the bus, his jeans unbuttoned, and I knew—I fucking knew!—what was going on.*

Bile rose in my throat and I turned away quickly before either could notice me. Tears burned my eyes as I ran across the parking lot and hailed another cab. Somehow I got out the name of the hotel we were staying in through the raking sobs shaking my body. The driver kept asking if I was okay, but I couldn't answer him. I wasn't.

I was definitely not okay and probably never would be again.

When the cab pulled up in front of the hotel, I tossed him all the cash I had in my pocket, not caring that the ride had cost less than twenty bucks, and I'd tossed him several hundred dollars. I stumbled out of the back and into the hotel where I was thankfully greeted by a different receptionist and was just barely able to get out what room I was in. "I lost my key," I told her in a trembling voice.

I didn't see the kindness in her eyes, didn't see the few guests as they passed, giving me questioning and sympathetic glances. It took less than a minute to get the new key and I found my way up to the eighteenth floor through tear-filled eyes and locked myself in the unused bedroom in the suite I'd been sharing with Wroth. There was no way I could lie on the same bed where he had kissed me so tenderly, touched me and brought me untold pleasure just hours ago.

For weeks now we'd been sleeping in the same bed, touching intimately, kissing passionately—but never actually making love. I'd been on cloud nine, not even really questioning why Wroth wouldn't let me touch him as he so often touched me. But now I did and I couldn't stop thinking about it. Just hours ago I'd begged him to let me taste him as he had been tasting me with his tongue. Instead of letting me, he had distracted me all over again as he had latched onto my sex with his talented mouth and brought me to yet another screaming release.

Shame washed over me, adding to my already breaking heart. He wouldn't let me touch him, but he would let a stranger, some silicone Barbie doll wannabe suck his dick...? The tears poured faster, my sobs so hard they made my body feel as if it were being torn apart from the inside out.

Why didn't he want me?

Wasn't I good enough?

Wasn't I beautiful enough?

For hours those thoughts filtered through my brain until I felt as if my head was going to explode. Wroth didn't come back to our suite, not that I had expected him to. He was probably balls deep in Miss Bouncy Boobs. When the sun started shining through my window, I was still crying.

The phone beside my bed began ringing but I ignored it. If anyone needed me they would have called my cellphone. Sighing, I reached out, searching the bed beside me for it to check and see what time it was. When I couldn't feel it, I checked my pockets and groaned when I realized I must have dropped it when I'd run away from the sight of Wroth and...

I rarely cursed but an entire rainbow of bad words left my mouth as I climbed out of bed. Figures I would lose my phone on top of everything else shitty that had happened the night before. Clenching my jaw, I decided I didn't care that my phone was gone, or that the new case that was on it had been one that Wroth had given me. The one with the pair of glittery ruby slippers on it. It had been a small surprise just weeks ago because he knew that I loved all things Wizard of Oz.

No, I was glad it was gone, I decided as I climbed into the shower to wash away all outward traces of my brokenness.

I wasn't ready to face anyone so I dressed and left the room. I walked the streets of Baltimore until I figured it was time to go over to the venue. Of course I'd heard that the streets of Baltimore were dangerous, but in that moment I didn't care if something happened to me. If it did, it still wouldn't hurt me as bad as what Wroth had done to me the night before.

I needed to help Harris with his homework and I was sure that Liam was going to be worried about me, so I finally hailed a cab. When I got there, no one even noticed that I'd been gone. They were all in a tizzy over the fight that Devlin and Zander had gotten into the night before.

For a moment I was able to push my own pain to the back of my mind and went in search of Natalie.

The deadness in her eyes was the only outward sign that Natalie wasn't her normal self. She walked with her head held high, her shoulders straight, and her jaw clenched. Her face was pale, making those blue-gray eyes stand out even more in her beautiful face. As soon as I saw her, I wrapped my arms around her. "Are you okay?"

Natalie hugged me back, her arms tight around me for a moment before stepping back and giving me a grim smile. "I'll get over it, but life goes on. He's not the only man in the universe."

"What happened?" I asked, having only heard that Zander had admitted to having a bet going on between Devlin and himself about who could have sex with Natalie first. Apparently a fight had broken out not long after and Natalie had been forced to call Emmie.

"They destroyed the club last night. I had to pay for ten grand in damages, not counting the booze they destroyed. So I had no choice but to call in the big guns since there were people who recognized Devlin and Zander and were

recording the whole thing on their phones. Emmie will be here tonight, to clean up my mess." Natalie's chin started trembling but then she gritted her teeth together and shook her head. "Look, Rissa. I don't want the reason for Dev and Z's fight to get back to my brothers. I might hate the very sight of those two jackasses right now, but I don't want them dead. Promise me you won't say anything to anyone."

If I had been Natalie, I would have called my brothers first and then helped pick out Devlin and Zander's caskets. That she was protecting them showed how much stronger a person she was than me. Giving a nod, I promised her I wouldn't say anything.

For the rest of the day I stayed in the dressing room with Harris, getting him caught up on school work so much that he finished a full week's work in one afternoon. He didn't seem to mind though, asking for another assignment each time we finished one. He was pissed off at his father for what he'd done to Natalie and needed the distraction of school just as much as I needed one.

Emmie arrived not long before OtherWorld was supposed to take the stage and I was glad for the added distraction of four-year-old Mia. I kept her entertained until it was time for bed and then tucked her in. After that I was left with nothing to do, since no one was awake to distract me and my pain came flooding back like a dam had been broken.

By some grace of God I had been able to avoid Wroth all day. I didn't even want to look at him, but knew that a confrontation with him was inevitable. Liam came back to the bus first. He gave me a small smile when he saw me. The smile disappeared when he saw the look on my face. I'd started crying again not long after Mia had fallen asleep and I hadn't been able to stop since that first damn tear had fallen.

"Rissa?" Liam's voice was full of concern and he dropped down beside me on the couch. "What's wrong? Are you okay? Are you sick?" He felt my forehead, his eyes troubled.

I couldn't lie to my brother, but I couldn't tell him what was wrong either. Not yet, maybe not ever. I wanted to hold onto at least a little of my pride. "I'm not sick," I assured him, wiping at my tear-streaked face only for more tears to fall. "I don't want to talk about it, Li."

His eyes turned stormy. "Did Wroth do something?" I couldn't help but flinch at the sound of Wroth's name and my brother's eyes went a little wild. "What did he fucking do, Rissa?"

"It's nothing. He didn't do anything that he didn't have the right to." More pain and shame filled me because it was the truth. For the last few weeks while Wroth and I had been getting closer, while I'd let him learn every secret that my body had to give, we had never said one word about being exclusive. And while my brother and Wroth might have tried their hardest to keep me innocent of what the rock world was like, I wasn't *a complete idiot. And one of the biggest rules I'd learned that the majority of them had was that rockers didn't do exclusivity. They liked their freedom and Wroth still had his.*

Liam must have seen exactly how much I was hurting, how deep the pain was, because he didn't say another word. Just wrapped me up in his arms like he had always done when I was a little girl and rocked me back and forth for the longest time, softly humming the lullaby that Mary Beth had always sang to us as kids. He didn't release me until the door of the bus opened.

I knew who it was without having to lift my head. I'd always had some sixth sense where he was concerned. Liam went stone still against me, his anger at his cousin evident in every hard line of his handsome face. I clung to him a little tighter for a moment, trying to steal some of his strength before I forced myself to finally look at the man behind me.

When I finally met his gaze, his espresso eyes were full of concern. "Rissa, what's wrong?"

"What the fuck did you do to her?" Liam demanded, stepping around me so that he stood between me and Wroth, protecting me as he always had.

"Me?" Wroth's eyes narrowed on my brother. "I haven't even seen her since last night. I-"

"Li, it's okay." I touched his back and he turned to face me. "I need to talk to Wroth. Alone."

"Rissa..." I clenched my jaw, refusing to argue with him, and he muttered a curse. "Okay, fine. But if you need me call me."

"I can't," I bit my bottom lip. "I lost my cellphone somewhere last night."

"I have your phone," Wroth said as he pulled it out of his back pocket. "You must have dropped it in the parking lot..." He broke off when I quickly turned away. A sob bubbled up, trying to break free, but I bit my lip to keep it at bay; biting so hard that I actually tasted blood. "Liam, get out," Wroth suddenly snarled, letting me know loud and clear that he knew exactly what was wrong with me now.

Liam didn't leave immediately and I could imagine the stare down that both big men were having behind me, but I didn't dare turn around to see if I was right. Tears continued to fall. I didn't want him to see me like this. Didn't want to have yet another reason to be ashamed, but there was no way I could stop them.

"You'd better not hurt her again," Liam growled as he stormed off the bus.

It wasn't until the door was slammed behind my brother that Wroth moved. When I felt his hands touch my shoulders I jerked away and turned to face him, unable to handle his hands on me right then. "Don't," I cried. "Don't touch me ever again."

"Marissa..." His face was full of strain now, his eyes pleading with me. "What did you see?"

"Enough to know I mean nothing to you." The sob started to bubble up again and I swallowed it down. *"Have you been doing that this whole time?"* I demanded, my anger growing by the second. *"Do you get me off and then go let your groupies finish what you won't let me..?"*

He grabbed my arms, ignoring my flinch as I tried to pull away. *"No, sweetheart. No, never. It wasn't like that."* His voice was rougher than I'd ever heard it. He pulled me against him, one hand wrapping around my hair and pulling my head against his chest. I felt his lips in my hair, felt his trembling hands. *"I'm so sorry, Rissa. So damn sorry."*

My eyes closed, taking a deep breath, inhaling the scent of him that I loved so much. This man had destroyed me, had broken me to the point that I didn't know if I would ever be able to put myself back together again. So why did I care if his hands trembled, if his voice was full of pained emotion?

I jerked away from him, unable to handle being so close when I was hurting so badly. *"Just go, Wroth. I can't... I just can't be around you right now."*

For a moment, just a small moment, I thought he was going to protest and demand that we talk about this. If he had I wasn't sure what would have happened. Maybe I would have broken down and fallen at his feet, demanding to know why he couldn't want me like he had so obviously wanted Miss Bouncy Boobs last night. Perhaps I would have let him make up some kind of excuse, that what I'd seen had been just a trick of the light and he hadn't been getting his dick *sucked by some skanky-ass slut last night. Or maybe, just maybe I would have gone all ninja on him and kicked his ass for breaking my heart.*

But he didn't, and those maybes were just that. Maybes. He grabbed his stuff and left the bus.

I went to bed and cried myself into a deep, exhausted sleep...

* * *

Tears burned my eyes and I blinked them back, wishing I could blink away the memories just as easily. I looked at Wroth across the table spread out with an array of Italian food. I still loved him. Still needed him, wanted him just as much now as I did then. "Why wasn't I enough for you, Wroth? Why couldn't you want me?"

"Mari-" He tried to speak, but I didn't want to hear what he had to say now any more than I had back then.

"You hurt me so much," I whispered.

"I know, sweetheart. I know and all I can say is that I'm sorry. Just listen for a minute and let me tell you about that night."

"I can't." I wasn't ready, not by a long shot, to hear him tell me about that night. I knew what I'd seen and it was burned forever into my mind.

It still didn't stop me from loving him so desperately. Which meant that I had to make a choice. Could I forgive him and move on with him? Or did I hold onto the pain and anger and everything else and stay buried in the past?

CHAPTER 17

WROTH

The food in front of me lost its appeal as I watched the pain fill Marissa's eyes. I knew that she must have been reliving the night she had found me with the chick that had blindsided me with her drunken… Well there was no other way to describe it but to call it an attack. I grimaced, that night and the following coming flashing back.

The pain that had been on Marissa's face that night she had thrown me out of her life was like a dagger to my heart. I had hurt the one person I never wanted to hurt. Her pain had left me gasping like someone had slit my throat. Even now, as I watched tears fill those pretty eyes I loved so much, I felt as if someone were choking me.

I couldn't look at her and keep from drowning in her pain. Pain that I was responsible for.

The waiter appeared beside our table and he had to clear his throat a few times before I could force myself to look up at him. "Can I get you two anything else?"

I shook my head. "Just the bill."

"Of course." He pulled something from his apron and sat the little black book on the table. I didn't even open it. Just pulled out my wallet, tossed down the first two bills I came to, and then reached for Marissa's hand. The waiter made a choking, stuttering sound when he picked the book up again, but I ignored him.

"Let's go, sweetheart." Even white teeth sunk into her luscious bottom lip, but she didn't protest.

Thankfully we didn't have to wait long for a cab outside the little restaurant. One pulled up almost immediately. As soon as we were inside, I pulled her head onto my shoulder. Her tears soaked through my shirt, but I just let her cry. Marissa hated how much Liam and I—as well at the rest of our friends—tried to shield her, but she needed it. She has always had a sensitive soul and always would, no matter how much she tried to harden herself against the world, she would always need protecting. That didn't make her a weak woman in my eyes. It made her exactly what my own world-wary soul needed.

The bus was still empty when we got back. I carried Marissa on board and then down the hall to the large bathroom. She was still silently crying, and each tear was like another slice of the dagger already lodged into my heart. If she kept this up I wasn't going to live through the day.

My girl didn't protest as I stripped her of her clothes. My body, already hard from having had her in my arms, throbbed as I unveiled her gorgeous curves. I pushed my need for her down with a force that left me shaking. She needed for me to take care of her, not take advantage of her vulnerability.

The last of her clothes fell to the floor and I couldn't help but stare down at her beauty for a moment longer before stepping away from her to turn on the shower. The bathroom quickly filled with steam and I shrugged out of my own clothes before lifting her and stepping into the shower stall with her.

Trembling hands wrapped around my waist, her body going lax from the heat of the shower pouring down over us both. I bent my head and kissed away all of her tears. When you showered on a tour bus, you didn't have the pleasure of taking as long as you wanted. The hot water only last so long before it got tepid, but I gave her another moment to enjoy it before reaching for her shampoo.

I'd never considered washing someone else's hair as an erotic experience, but then again I'd never washed anyone else's hair but my own. Bathing with someone was too personal an act, one that I'd only ever had the desire to do with one person. Her. During our all too brief relationship, I'd taken baths with her often, but never actually washed her. The feel of her hair, lathered with the sweet scent of her shampoo that invaded my senses, sent my body from hard and throbbing to pulsating with a need that was making standing a miracle.

A sexy little moan escaped her as I messaged her scalp. "Harder," she murmured in a voice hoarse from crying.

I rubbed harder, paying attention to the tension that was still knotted up in her neck. It wasn't until her head fell forward onto my chest that I rinsed her hair. Her arms tightened even more around my waist as I applied her conditioner, my fingers combing through the tangled length until I was satisfied.

The water was already cooling by the time I'd rinsed the conditioner from her hair, forcing me to rush through washing her body. I didn't get to take my time as I rubbed her loofah over her luscious body. I wished I could have had more time. I would have worshipped every inch of her body. Would have taken the time to appreciate how perfectly her light coloring went with my tanned complexion.

I used her loofah and body wash to wash myself and then rinsed us both before turning off the water. I smelled like honey and milk, but I didn't care. It was kind of soothing to have a scent that I associated with Marissa clinging to my skin.

Grabbing two towels from the linen cabinet beside the shower, I wrapped her hair with one and then began drying her. Unlike in the shower, I took my time, wiping away each drop of water slowly. It was sweet torture, and I knew from the way Marissa kept glancing up at me through her lashes, by the way her nipples had hardened and her tits had plumped, that she was just as affected as I was. When I crouched in front of her to dry her legs, the scent of her arousal nearly dropped me to my knees in my need to spread her folds and tongue her until she was dripping her release down my throat.

I clenched my jaw harder, feeling one of my fillings protest as I forced my attention on the task at hand. I wasn't going to take advantage of her. If I touched her right now, she would probably hate me for it later.

Once she was dry, I roughly rubbed the towel over my own body and then lifted her into my arms once again. "Wroth?" she whispered.

"What is it, sweetheart?" I stopped in front of her roost and pulled her nightgown out from under her pillow.

"Why did you have to break your promise?"

I closed my eyes, another slice of that dagger cutting my heart open. I'd promised not to touch another chick, and for one insane minute I'd broken that promise. How could I have fucked up so badly in just sixty seconds? "It was the biggest mistake of my life. One that I will never repeat." I cupped her face with my hand. "I swear that I'll never break your heart again, Mari. You are everything that is good in my world. Without you, nothing else matters. I'll spend the rest of my life proving it to you if I have to."

Her gaze lowered to the floor, her chin trembling once again. "I want to be with you... But—"

"I know," I murmured, kissing her temple. "You need time to trust me again. It's okay, Mari. I'll give you all the time you need. As long as there is even a small chance that you can forgive me one day, I don't mind the wait. I'll wait for you until the sun goes dark if I have to."

Marissa didn't respond, and I wasn't sure if I'd been expecting her to or not. She needed time, and I had plenty of that. Setting her on her feet, I slipped her gown over her head and then placed her into her roost before climbing in beside her. Her damp hair was cool against my bare chest as I pulled her closer. My aching dick was standing at attention so I pulled the covers up over us to hide it. Out of sight, out of mind, right?

I wished.

Within a matter of minutes Marissa's breathing evened out and she was asleep. I continued to lie there, in my own tortured paradise as I soaked up the feel of her in my arms. It seemed like an entire lifetime passed before my aching dick went down even a little. As the evening wore on, I heard the others returning. Heard some of them laughing, some of them arguing. With a sigh I closed my eyes, unable to fight the exhaustion that was starting to consume me.

***

The feel of soft fingers on my stomach jerked me awake. The ache in my dick that had still been there when I'd finally fallen asleep was ten times worse when I felt those soft fingertips tickle across my lower abdomen and one single digit skim the dampness on the head of my dick. I bit my lip, trying to keep back the groan that was building up in my chest, but was unable to keep it back when her fingers continued their journey downward and cupped my balls.

"Good morning," Marissa murmured in a sleep-husky voice that was possibly the sexiest sound known to man. "I was wondering when you were going to wake up."

Blue eyes twinkled in the dim lighting coming through the curtains of the roost. A hint of a smile teasing at the corners of her lips. The breakdown from yesterday still lingered in her gaze, but I also saw forgiveness. Marissa had always been such a forgiving person, but what I'd done—what she still thought I had done—was something most women would never be able to forgive. That she could forgive me without an explanation showed me just how strong she was.

"I love you, Mari." The words were easier to say than I thought they would be, making me wonder why I hadn't been able to say them until that moment. Fuck, I'd been such a pussy by not telling her how much she meant to me. Never again.

The twinkle in those blue eyes grew brighter, even white teeth sinking into a lip that had already been tortured enough the day before. I cupped her face in both hands, rubbing one thumb over her lips until she released her hold on it. "Don't you believe me?"

Swallowing hard, she nodded. "Y-yes. I believe you. I'm just trying to figure out if I'm still asleep or not. Maybe I'm dreaming…"

"No dream, sweetheart. Here, let me prove it to you." Before she could open her mouth again, I rolled her onto her back and sealed her lips with my own. Her legs spread willingly and I settled between them with a growl of contentment. The heat of her arousal burned through the ridiculously thin layer of her nightgown, scalding my dick as it rubbed over her folds. Marissa trembled, her fingers sinking into my hair in a silent plea to deepen the kiss.

It was times like this, when I had the taste of her on my tongue, the feel of her luscious body enfolding me against her own, that I could understand why Liam had gotten so addicted to his drugs. Marissa was my own form of heroin, coke, meth. The feel of her in my arms, her lips kissing me back, the scent of her arousal as I thrust against her clit was like a drug that I would have killed to have an endless supply of. The strangled little sounds she was making, the way her nails raked over my scalp, the fucking softness of her body as her legs wrapped around my waist and she arched her back to get closer pushed my arousal higher and higher until I knew that I wasn't going to last.

With a curse, I broke the kiss and pulled back just enough to get her gown over her head. I was so far gone I didn't have the sense to appreciate the view as inch by inch her incredible body was exposed to me. My hands went straight for her amazing tits. The need to taste her ripe little nipples was overwhelming and I sucked one into my mouth. Marissa gasped, her back arching, her nails once more scraping over my scalp as she held me against her.

My dick developed a mind of its own, twitching against her open thighs, dripping pre-cum onto her mound. My balls tightened, letting me know loud and clear that I wasn't going to last long. My breathing was ragged, my heart pounding against my chest in a way that it only did when I was about to come. With a groan, I lifted my head from Marissa's tits and kissed my way down her body.

The strangled sounds she had just been making turned into little mewling sounds as I latched onto her clit with my lips. If the taste of Marissa's skin and lips were my drug of chose, the decadent taste of her pussy on my tongue was the sweet nectar of ambrosia that the gods themselves lived off of. I'd never tasted anything as good as Marissa's pussy, something I'd made a meal of on a regular basis before our relationship had went to hell.

"Wroth…" My name came out a gasp, her thighs trembling. I could tell just by the little sounds she was making that she was close. "I'm… No, please," she protested when I lifted my head.

My face was wet with her essence. I licked my lips, savoring her juices. "Come here," I commanded. I sat back against her pillows, having to slouch more than a little because the roost was so small.

She didn't question me, didn't hesitate, but simply did as I asked. I grasped my excruciatingly aching dick in one hand and cupped her ass with the other, pulling her closer. Her thighs spread wide for me and I guided my dick to her opening, skimming it over her glistening folds. Marissa threw her head back, her hair spilling over her shoulders and my own as she reached out to steady herself with her soft hands on my chest.

I buried my face in her chest, licking the valley between her tits as I stroked myself over her opening and up to her clit, then back again. She was growing close again, and I was right behind her. With a groan that sounded animalistic to my own ears I pushed her onto her back and dipped my tip inside her scalding hot, tight little body. Her eyes widened with a mixture of surprise and passion. "Wroth!" she cried in the next moment, her body convulsing around me as she came apart all over my dick.

It physically hurt, but I quickly pulled from her just as my own release jetted forward, spraying across her still quivering stomach. With a sated groan, I dropped down onto her, crushing her beneath me, rubbing my semen into the both of us.

For long moments I lay there, her soft fingertips caressing up and down my back while our breathing slowly evened out. I wanted to stay right there, with her in my arms, her come still dripping onto the sheets beneath us, for the rest of our lives…

The pounding on the wall beside Marissa's roost had my head snapping up, the urge to murder never more powerful than in that moment. "What?" I bellowed.

"Er…" I heard Zander snicker on the other side of the curtain and my irritation heightened. "If you have finished defiling Rissa, you might want to come out and explain your intentions to her brother. Liam's about to go off the rails after hearing that award-winning performance, dude."

Marissa made a distressed sound, her hands leaving my back to cover her flaming face. I wasn't worried about Liam. I could deal with him later. But Zander was going to pay for embarrassing my girl. My arm shot through the curtain of the roost and grabbed him by the throat. "You go tell Liam I'll be out when I'm good and ready. But first, apologize to Marissa."

I felt Zander's throat move as he swallowed. He was the goof ball of the five of us, but he knew when he had crossed a line with me. And he had just crossed the biggest line of all. "Sorry, Rissa," he called through the curtain. No way was I going to let him stick his head inside and see her deity-worthy nakedness.

His apology didn't satisfy me but I released him. My gaze went straight to Marissa's red face. That blush was adorable on her, but I hated the reason for it. With her in my arms, I'd forgotten that we were on some highway traveling at over seventy miles an hour with a bus full of people that would be all too amused with the show we had just put on for them. The one thing I'd learned fast about rockers? They could be very juvenile at times. Zander was possibly the biggest one of all, but I couldn't kill him for it. At least that was what I kept telling myself.

"I'm sorry, sweetheart. I forgot that people were around and could actually hear us," I said.

Slowly Marissa dropped her hands, shaking her head at the roost above us. The smile on her face caught me completely off guard though. I hadn't seen that particular smile, the one that was so full of life and love and perfection, in so long. It caused my heart to clench, remembering that I was the reason why it hadn't been present in so long. "I'm curious to know what you plan on telling Li. What *are* your intentions, Wroth Niall?"

I couldn't help but snort at her question. I had a million and one intentions and a million of them required a bed and privacy. The remaining one… Well, I was a little old school when it came to that remaining one. I needed to talk to Liam first and then and only then would I tell her.

CHAPTER 18

WROTH

I was still feeling sated from my morning with Marissa when I walked backstage with my bandmates later that night, getting ready for the concert. Demon's Wings was still on stage. Nik was getting the fans riled up, knowing that getting them to chant their name would get Axton's blood pumping.

Emmie appeared from the side of the stage, one arm holding onto her clip board while she texted rapidly with her free hand. "You guys ready?" she asked, only looking up from her phone once she had hit send. Her eyes went to Axton first and she rolled her big green eyes at him. "Get over it, Ax. He gets off on pissing you off when you close the show."

"One more song!" Nik shouted on stage.

Twenty thousand fans screamed so loudly that the stage vibrated. The first note coming from Drake's Fender filled the air, and the screaming suddenly quietened as he started with a solo that produced goose bumps on my own arms.

Emmie glanced back out on stage, smiled happily and then turned to go. I caught her elbow as she started to walk away. Her eyes widened when she looked up at me. "Hey," she said and grinned. "What's up?"

"Can you do something for me?" If possible, her eyes widened even more. Yeah, I didn't normally seek out her help, but there were things that I wanted done that I just didn't know how to accomplish. It was a first for me. I wanted this perfect though, and Emmie could move mountains when she had to.

"Of course," she readily agreed. "What do you need?"

I glanced back at my bandmates and grimaced. I didn't want nor need the grief they would give me if they overheard what I needed Emmie to do. "Can you wait for me after the show? I need it done in the next few weeks. Definitely before we get to Kansas."

Emmie nodded. "I'll be waiting right here," she promised.

The fans were still chanting Demon's Wings' name when we stepped onto stage after it was turned over and we did another quick sound check. For the next hour we performed, and I played for the masses as they turned from chanting Demon's Wings to OtherWorld within the span of one song. If Drake had ended with a guitar solo, then I was sure as hell going to start with one.

When it was over I was soaked with sweat. The lights that shone down on us throughout a show were worse than the noon sun in the desert. The stage was littered with red roses, panties and bras, and pieces of paper that professed fans' love and desire for us. The roses were all picked up, but no one bothered to pick up the underwear or the love letters. Zander was the only single one of us now, and he'd never been one for collecting bras and panties. He'd rarely ever hooked up at concerts, but always went out afterwards to local clubs or bars to find someone to spend the night with.

Like always, Axton didn't speak after the concert was over. His throat was probably a ball of fire after that last song. I carefully handed my favorite Fender over to Pock, the roadie who was in charge of taking care of my guitars, and stepped off stage. Emmie was standing right where I'd left her with her phone to one ear. Green eyes were narrowed as she listened to whoever was on the other end of the call.

I stood back, not wanting to interrupt her. I might have stood a good foot over her, and outweighed her by a hundred-plus pounds but she still terrified the shit out of me. One glare from those startling green eyes and she could freeze me in my tracks. She had more balls than any man I'd ever met, more intelligence than most people would ever dream of having. Emmie Armstrong was one of the most trusted names in the rock-n-roll world, and she was also one of the most feared if you happened to be on her shit list.

"He says he's who, again, Rachel?" Emmie asked, her eyes darkening when she paused to listen again. "Okay... No. Don't worry about him. I'm just surprised it's taken him this long to figure out where she was. If he's smart, the man will catch up with us before much longer. No... Just get me more candidates for nannies... Because once he shows up, Felicity might decide that she wants to go home."

My own eyes widened at the mention of Emmie's nanny's name. Felicity was like one of the Demon's Wings' family. Everyone seemed to love her. So who the hell was going to show up and take her away? As soon as Emmie lowered her phone with a frustrated sigh, I stepped forward. "Is Felicity okay?" I liked the chick myself. She was sweet but also feisty. She didn't take shit from anyone. Not even Emmie.

"She's okay. Just someone from her family is looking for her." She stuffed her phone in her back pocket, muttering under her breath. "Fucking bikers," I thought she said but wasn't sure.

"What?"

Another sigh left her. "Nothing. It was nothing." A small smile lifted the corners of her lips. "So, what can I do for you, big guy?"

It took a little while, but I finally told Emmie everything I needed her to get and do for me before we made it to Kansas in a few weeks. After my talk with Liam that morning, I wanted to make Marissa's experience at that particular stop on our tour something she would remember for the rest of our lives together. She wasn't happy about at least one of the things I'd asked of her, but she was grinning up at me when she walked away.

I made my way back to the OtherWorld bus, hoping to find Marissa on board and alone. Of course she wasn't and I gritted my teeth when I saw that it was full of rockers that weren't my bandmates. All I wanted was a quiet night, damn it. A few of the Trance guys were sitting around the living room while Bishop and Drew from Alchemy were standing in the kitchenette fixing themselves large paper plates of pizza, wings and breadsticks. Zander was sitting at the kitchenette table with Linc, Liam and Kenzie. Marissa, however was nowhere in sight.

"Rissa not back from watching the kids?" I asked as I grabbed a slice of meat lovers' pizza and taking a hungry bite of it.

"She said to let you guys know that she would be a little longer. She was still talking to Lana and Dallas when I left," Kenzie let me know.

I picked up another slice of pizza and turned without another word, heading back off the bus. I wasn't sure which bus the kids had been taken to tonight, but I would knock on all of the doors until I found my girl. I'd been away from her for long enough as it was.

I reached Lana and Drake's bus first and knocked once before someone called for me to come in. I climbed up the steps and stuck my head into the living room. Shane, Drake, and Nik were sitting around the room with cartons of Chinese in their hands. "You fuckers seen Marissa?"

"She's over at Jesse's bus," Drake informed me with a mouth full of chicken and broccoli. I nodded and started to leave. "Hey, wait. Don't rush off. The girls were still deep into some conversation about who the fuck knows when we left them over half an hour ago. Sit and eat with us, man."

I stuffed the last bite of my pizza into my mouth and shrugged. I was still hungry enough to eat an entire pizza by myself, and knowing Marissa she would be over there talking for half the night. It wouldn't matter if I showed up to take her back to our bus or not, she would be there until the girls got talked out. I took the carton of noodles that Nik held out and dropped down onto the couch beside him. Sports Center was on and I accepted the bottle of beer Shane handed over before settling in to have a little guy-time with my friends. "You okay with this?" I asked Drake as I tipped the bottle at him.

Drake shrugged. "Dude, I haven't touched a drop of booze in years. I can control myself if you fuckers have a beer or two."

CHAPTER 19

MARISSA

L ana hid a yawn behind her hand before rubbing it over her stomach. "Okay. I really need to get back to my bus. Neveah is probably already asleep and Drake is going to throw a fit when he realizes I'm not in bed with him. I'm really surprised he hasn't been blowing up my phone or come over here to get me."

Dallas, sitting across from me, glanced down at her phone. "Shit, is that really the time?" She groaned. "Axton and Cannon left hours ago and I told him I'd be right behind him."

I laughed, noticing how late it was for the first time in several hours. It was nearly three in the morning and we'd been sitting in Layla and Jesse's bus since before eleven talking about random things. It felt good to just sit and talk to my girlfriends—something that I hadn't had a lot of when I was growing up. "I'd better head back too. I bet OtherWorld's bus is a disaster." I knew that Natalie had ordered enough pizzas to feed an army and then told everyone that dinner was waiting for them on our bus. I was just surprised that security hadn't come knocking because they had gotten too rowdy. They must have been good little rock stars over there.

Layla stood, pulling her hair back into a messy bun after stretching tired muscles. "It's been a long day, ladies. Love you little bitches, but I'm going to bed."

"I'd have headed to bed when the bald beast had if I had that waiting on me, Lay," Dallas said, smirking up at her.

The smaller, curvy woman sighed. "I'm mad at him at the moment so he hasn't been getting any."

I gasped along with the other two women at Layla's confession. "What the fuck?" Lana exclaimed. "What did he do?"

She grimaced. "I want to have another baby and he won't even talk about it. He can't get over what happened with the boys' birth. But he won't listen to me when I tell him that that was just one of those things. For the love of gods, did you see what I had kicking around inside of me when they were first born? Of course I went into labor two months early. And that electrolyte thing can be monitored. I've talked until I'm blue in the face about it and he ignores me. I can just say the word baby and he gets up and leaves."

Lana stared at her sister as if she had lost her mind. I'd only heard about how crazy things had been when Layla had gone into preterm labor with the twins. She had been out for more than two days and the doctors had been worried that she wasn't going to wake up after having to be put under for an emergency C-section. It turned out that she had had a major electrolyte deficiency and once the doctors had gotten that straightened out she had woken up soon after. But I could honestly understand where Jesse was coming from. That must have been a nightmare.

"Layla, you were out for over two days. What we went through—what that man back there in that bedroom went through—while you wouldn't wake up was one of the worst times in our lives. You can't expect him to want to even chance going through that again." When her sister just glared at her, Lana stood and hugged the shorter woman. "We love you, Layla. Without you no one would survive. You having another baby would be a beautiful thing, but like Jesse, I would be a basket case the entire pregnancy. Don't be mad at him for being scared of losing you."

Layla hung her head. "Okay. I guess I really didn't understand how hard it was on you guys." Her chin trembled. "I just…the twins are getting older and I guess I have baby fever with you and now Dallas pregnant."

"Don't go spreading that fever around, girl," I murmured, not wanting that particular ailment anytime soon. I was lucky enough to have the change to get pregnant if the urge ever hit, but it would take a lot of work to achieve it. I'd had eggs harvested before my chemo treatments when I was teenager, something that had been more than a little controversial since I'd been so young at the time. Surprisingly, it had been Wroth who had made it possible for me to have the eggs harvested, paying for another doctor to come in from France just to have the procedure done. "I don't need that crap right now."

Dallas stood and grabbed my hand. "Okay, you two. It's late and now Layla is going to go back there and fuck her man, because he's hot and she isn't mad at him anymore." The other two women laughed, breaking the tension that had filled the room just moments ago. "And I'm going to go over to my bus and fuck mine. So let's go, bitches."

I hugged Layla and followed my friends off the bus, fighting a yawn of my own. Lana and I said goodnight to Dallas outside her bus before heading on down the row of buses. We passed the darkened bus that belonged to Shane and Harper, and then stopped outside of Lana's. "Good night, Rissa." Lana kissed my cheek and opened the door of her bus. I waved and headed toward OtherWorld's bus when I heard the male laughter coming from the living room of Lana's bus, picking up the sound of Wroth's rough laugh easily.

Lana stuck her head inside quickly before turning back to me. "Come on in, girl. It doesn't look like this bunch is going to leave anytime soon."

Frowning, I stepped onto the bus and found four rockers spread around the living room, beers in three of the four's hands while they watched

World's Dumbest on television. There were empty cartons of Chinese food littering the side tables and the place smelled like a college student's dorm room. Lana stood there in the middle of them, hands on her hips as she frowned at the mess in her living room. "You fuckers are cleaning this up before you go home."

"Aw, sis. You know we will." Shane tipped his beer at her. "Can you get me another beer?"

Lana gave him a death glare. "Get it yourself, you slob." Her gaze went to Drake and her eyes softened. "Did you save me any noodles?"

Drake held out his hands to her and she climbed onto his lap. "In the microwave, Angel." He pulled her closer, burying his face in her neck. "Shane, get Angel her food." Grumbling, Shane stood and went into the kitchenette to grab himself another beer—the last of them by the looks of it—and a carton of Chinese.

I let my eyes travel around the room as I stood there wondering if I should just go back to my own bus. Nik was sitting on the couch with Wroth, his ice blue eyes smiling at me as he lifted his Corona to his lips and took another swallow. I smiled back, because it was hard not to do so when you had that dream of a man flashing that killer smile at you. I might have been stupidly in love with Wroth Niall, but I'd always had a small crush on Nik. What woman wouldn't crush a little on a man who looked like a yummy bad boy but acted like a true Prince Charming?

I knew that Wroth's eyes were on me, could feel the fire in his gaze like a physical caress as it skimmed over me from head to toe and back again. I kept my own eyes away from him, however, feeling oddly shy.

One of the reasons I'd stayed so long over at Layla's bus talking to my friends was because of him. I didn't know how to handle myself around him at the moment. Waking up in his arms, followed by one of the most amazing foreplay sessions known to man, had left me feeling vulnerable. When I'd woken up with him beside me that morning, I'd just lain there watching him sleep for the longest time. My heart had ached more and more with each passing moment as I'd fought an internal battle with myself.

Could I forgive him? Damn it, hadn't I already done so?

If I were being honest with myself, then the answer was simple. Yes, I had forgiven him. We had not made any promises of exclusivity, not really. It might have hurt—still hurt—but he hadn't been mine when he'd cheated on me. This time around I wanted things to be different. I wanted him to make promises, wanted to know that he was mine and only mine if we went any further.

I just didn't know how to ask for it without further humiliating myself.

Nik scooted over on the couch, making room between himself and Wroth. With a wink, he patted the seat next to him. "Come sit with us,

Rissa. We could use a hot chick to even out the testosterone stinking up the place."

"It does stink in here," Lana muttered around a bite of the noodles she was pushing into her mouth with her chopsticks. "Does it smell this bad over at your bus, Rissa?"

"Worse," I assured her with a laugh as I took the offered seat between Nik and Wroth.

As soon as I sat down, Nik draped an arm around my shoulders and Wroth made a growl in protest. "You wanna lose that arm, bro?"

Nik chuckled, not scared of Wroth's threat. "I'll take my chances." He winked down at me again and I couldn't help but grin back. "How you been, gorgeous? I feel like we've barely gotten to talk since the tour started. Em says you're doing a great job with the kids. And, thanks, by the way. Apparently I'm adding a freakin' dog to my family this Christmas because of you and that damn *Wizard of Oz* movie."

"So Mia gets her Toto?"

"Have I ever not given my baby what she wants?" Nik grimaced. "I should probably stop spoiling her so much. She's going to be as bad as her momma before long."

"What planet do you live on?" Drake demanded. "She already is."

Shane grunted his agreement. "Worse. I never put on tiaras and played princess tea party with Emmie when she was Mia's age."

"You didn't just admit that," Wroth snorted. "Are there pictures?"

"None that you'll ever see, bro." Shane took his seat once again and crossed his legs. "Better watch out. You spend more than ten minutes in the same room with Mia and you'll have a sparkly tiara, plastic clip-on earrings, and lipstick too."

"Lipstick!" I giggled at the picture that Shane had just put in my head. It was hard enough to imagine big, beautiful Shane Stevenson playing dress-up like that, but now to picture Wroth in the same position? I laughed so hard tears slipped from my eyes. "What color?"

"Mia's favorite color is peach," Nik commented. "It makes Shane's eyes sparkle."

"Shut up, fucker."

For the next hour that was how our night went. The Demon's Wings guys tossed out snarky comments about each other, calling each other names, but you could tell that they loved and respected each other. The four Demons were more brothers than bandmates. They had always had each other's backs, no matter what. There was more love in their strange family-by-choice than I'd ever seen in one that was family by blood.

During that time, I could feel Wroth's tension. He was waiting for a sign from me to leave. I was torn between wanting to stay and hang out with our friends and leaving so that we could have some alone time. Thoughts of our morning together made me squirm a little as I sat there beside him, feeling the heat that was burning the entire left side of my body where it brushed against his.

Eventually I couldn't stop from yawning and Wroth jumped up, taking me with him. "Time for bed, sweetheart."

"Goodnight, Rissa," the guys called as I silently waved goodbye.

"Don't forget that movie night is at my bus this weekend," Lana called after me.

I made a face at her. "Nothing in the horror genre, if you please." Lana and Harper both had a thing for scary movies, but I couldn't stomach them. And being scared was my least favorite emotion to feel.

Lana pouted. "You're no fun."

"I'll bring a few to choose from," I told her, ignoring the pout. "How about *Charlie and the Chocolate Factory*?"

"No!" Lana shook her head adamantly. "No way. You want to talk about scary? Nothing freaks me out more than seeing that sexy-ass man like...*that*." She shuddered. "Anything but that."

I laughed and waved again before following Wroth off the bus.

The air was humid but there was the hint of rain on the soft breeze. I inhaled deeply as I walked down the row of buses, enjoying one of my favorite scents. If I'd been back on the farm with the promise of rain in the air, I would open my bedroom window and wait for the rain to come before letting it lull me into a deep, peaceful sleep.

Strong arms suddenly wrapped around my waist from behind, making me gasp in a mixture of surprise and delight. My shyness came back twice as bad and I leaned my head back against Wroth's chest. His jaw was deliciously rough with his evening beard as he kissed my neck, making me shiver.

"I love our friends, Mari, but you were starting to kill me in there," his sexy voice rumbled against my ear. "And if you let Nik Armstrong put his arm around you like that one more time, it's going to be your fault when Emmie suddenly has a one-armed husband."

I couldn't help the giggle that escaped me at his threat and turned in his arms, my shyness fading as I wrapped my arms around him and buried my face in his chest. "Poor Nik," I laughed. "But I doubt that having only one arm would distract from his sexiness."

Wroth tensed and I knew I'd just woken up the jealous rage monster that had been simmering for the last hour while I'd sat next to another man who had teasingly flirted with me. I wanted to laugh at the idea of Nik ever having romantic or sexual thoughts of me. His ice blue eyes only saw Emmie and that wasn't likely to ever change. But that didn't matter to Wroth right then.

I had to admit that I liked that he was jealous. That he hated the mere idea of someone else touching me...or that I considered another man sexy. It was adorable, really.

"You think Nik is sexy?" His voice was low, but would have been no less powerful if he had roared.

I smirked up at him, my eyes twinkling with amusement. "I think a lot of guys are sexy, Wroth." A growl escaped him and I lifted my hands to cup his face. I couldn't see his eyes in the faint glow from a distant street light, but I could tell from the way his forehead was scrunched up that he was glowering down at me. "That doesn't mean I want them. I only want one sexy rocker touching me, honey."

"I love you, Marissa."

My heart melted at those words. When he'd first said them to me just the morning before, I'd been stunned by them, unable to believe I was actually awake and hearing those treasurable words that I'd always hoped to hear from him. But I'd never imagined that he would say them again. Wroth just wasn't the vocal type. I'd figured that he had said them once and that was most likely all I would ever get. To have him say them again, to have those three little words that could heal or cripple a person spoken by this man was truly a miracle in his own right.

And I didn't know how to respond to them. I knew instinctively that he wanted me to say them back. We both knew that I loved him more than anything; it wasn't a secret that I'd ever tried to hide from him. But I couldn't utter them. They wouldn't even come when I opened my mouth to speak.

The pause was a short one, but it felt like it went on for eternity before he lowered his head and brushed his lips over my own in a kiss so soft that it brought tears to my eyes. "I love you, sweetheart," he breathed against my lips. "Let's go to bed. I need to hold you tonight."

Swallowing around the lump of tears clogging my throat, I nodded and let him take my hand as we continued on to the bus that was our home for the next few months.

CHAPTER 20

MARISSA

"If one more person says the words 'milk jugs', I'm going to do bodily damage."

My eyes widened and went straight to Natalie who was sitting across from me at the sound of Dallas's angry voice just outside of our bus. She grimaced and shrugged. Tonight was our girls' night in and we were going to watch a movie while the guys went out and drank a few beers. Normally it was all the girls but tonight our group was going to be smaller since Lucy had a cold and Layla didn't want to leave her, and Emmie had to deal with a few issues with the venue for tomorrow night's concert. Kenzie had volunteered to help Felicity out with the children and they were watching their own G-rated movie on Emmie's bus tonight.

I wasn't sure who Dallas was talking to, but I did know what she was referring to. Since Dallas was pregnant again, she had had to give up nursing Cannon, but her already amazing breasts were larger than usual because of her new pregnancy. As were Lana's breasts that seemed to have grown another cup size just in the last two weeks. A few days ago I'd overheard several of the roadies talking about both women and calling their breasts 'milk jugs'. Since then it had been kind of an inside joke for the roadies.

I didn't know how Axton or Drake had reacted to hearing their wives' racks talked about in such a derogatory way, but Dallas was sure as heck making her opinion on it loud and clear at the moment. "You like your dick where it is, Pock? Keep laughing, motherfucker, and you'll be wearing it stapled to your fucking forehead."

The door to the bus opened and I bit my lip to keep from laughing as Dallas stepped into the living room. Her clear blue eyes were stormy, her face flushed with temper. Yeah, it really wouldn't help matters to burst out laughing just then. If there was anything I'd learned in the last few weeks of touring with her, it was that with Dallas's last pregnancy she was considerably much sweeter. Axton had joked that it was because she was having a boy and so as long as she had a little dick in her, she was okay. Now, he teased her repeatedly that they were going to have a girl. That was why she was twice the bitch at times. And twice the bitch did not bode well for the likelihood that Pock would finish the tour with his dick still attached to his body... Well, at least not to the part of his body it was supposed to be attached to.

"What was that, Pock?" Lana's voice could now be heard through the open door. "You wanna taste your own dick before she gets the staple gun? I can make it happen."

Natalie, hearing her sister-in-law's threat, groaned long and loud. "Just another thing to have to worry about. I know at least one of my brothers is going to end up in jail before the summer is over."

Outside there was a faint grumble in answer and Lana stepped onto the bus with Harper and Jenna right behind her. Jenna was laughing uncontrollably, and Harper was doing a little giggling of her own. Obviously neither had the same fear as I did about laughing at Dallas, or even Lana for that matter. Brave. They were very, very brave. When the door shut behind them Lana carefully sat down on the couch beside me, muttering a rainbow of colorful words under her breath.

Natalie handed out bowls of popcorn to the newcomers. "Who else was it?" she asked as she picked up the remote to the flat screen.

Dallas shrugged as she stuffed her mouth with salty, buttered popcorn. "Pock, Myles, Vance and Greg." She chewed, swallowed, then stuffed more in. "Don't worry about it, Nat. I'll deal with those pricks. They'd just better hope Axton doesn't get to them before I can."

"If Emmie hears them..." Natalie sighed, folding her legs back under the baggy sweatshirt she was wearing.

Harper snorted. "I wouldn't worry about Emmie hearing them. She was right behind us on her way to find Nik and Mia so that Mia could watch the movie with the other kids. If looks could kill, those four idiots would be burning in hell right now."

"The redhead will let me deal with them," Dallas assured Natalie. "Now turn on the movie, bitch. I came to watch male goodies shaking like they're hot."

I couldn't help but giggle at Dallas as she wiggled her brows suggestively. She had been the one to pick tonight's movie, *Magic Mike*. She and I had watched the movie together before, but it had been over a year since I'd seen Channing Tatum shaking his boys around.

"Shane does it better," Harper informed her best friend.

"Eww!" Jenna made a gagging sound and threw popcorn at her sister-in-law. "I seriously didn't need to know that."

"That's just…" Natalie made a face and shook her head. "No, just no. That's my brother."

"Drake doesn't shake his at me," Lana spoke up, rubbing her hands lovingly over her very large belly. There was a soft, dreamy look on her face and I just knew that she was fantasizing about her deliciously sexy husband. "He doesn't need to."

Harper raised a brow. "Shane doesn't *have* to shake it at me, but I never complain when he does." More gagging noises came from Jenna and

Natalie put her fingers in her ears, humming to herself to drown out the sound of their voices.

"Axton hasn't shaken his at me yet. Maybe I'll talk him into it tonight." Another handful of popcorn was stuffed into her mouth and she pouted down at her almost empty bowl. "Hey, you didn't give me very much."

I bit my lip to keep from reminding her that Natalie had given her the biggest bowl and that it had held nearly an entire bag of popcorn. Another difference between her current pregnancy and the last one was that she didn't have the morning sickness that she had experienced with Cannon. But her cravings had already set in and nothing salty stood a chance when she was around. Dallas didn't like it, though. The nurse in her suspected something was wrong, that her craving for salt meant that she needed the mineral. When Lana went in for her next appointment, something that Emmie had set up in a few of the cities we were stopping in for concerts and was necessary as Lana's pregnancy progressed, she was going to see the doctor as well. Her worry was that she was anemic and she wanted to make sure everything was going as it should.

"Here," Harper handed over her own bowl of popcorn. "I don't want it anyway."

"Thanks, Harp." Dallas blew her a kiss, then frowned. "Are you feeling okay? You look kind of pale."

I took a closer look at Harper, noticing not for the first time that the beautiful woman did look a little on the pale side. Her eyes had dark circles under them as well, making them appear almost bruised. The last two weeks hadn't been the easiest on her, that was for sure. After the refurbished bus had caught up with us, Harper, Shane, Jenna, Ranger and Harper's two bodyguards moved back onto it. Since then Harper wasn't allowed to go anywhere unless at least one of the bodyguards was able to go with her. I had little doubt that the two men were standing outside the OtherWorld bus right at that moment. Her privacy was basically obsolete now and would continue to be so until the person who had ransacked their bus was identified and taken care of. Since there were no leads, not even fingerprints, the likelihood of that happening anytime soon was pretty low.

The press had also caught wind of the incident, along with Ranger's injuries, and had been running an almost daily story regarding either something stupid from Shane's past, Harper's inability to conceive, or out and out lies that suggested that Harper and Shane were having problems and were headed for divorce. I didn't know how true the stories of Shane's past were, but I could guess from his constant clenched jaw that the tabloids had gotten at least some of it right. The stories about Harper and Shane having problems? That was the most ridiculous thing I'd ever heard. Shane was crazy about Harper, and even though I'd seen storm clouds in her uniquely violet eyes, she loved him just as much. Their relationship was strong, and it would take something a lot more damning than a few tell-all stories from women in Shane's past to destroy what they had.

"I'll be better when this tour is over and I can sleep in my own bed for a few nights and work in my own office instead of via freaking Skype." Harper curled her legs up under her and rested her head on Dallas's shoulder as the opening credits came on. "Don't worry about me, Dallas. I'm fine."

"Promise?" Dallas still looked concerned.

Harper sighed. "I promise."

For the next two and a half hours we watched the movie, having to pause more than a few times so that Lana could go pee. I was sure that anyone outside of the OtherWorld bus was getting a show of their own. We weren't quiet as we whooped and yelled and encouraged the very sexy men on screen to 'take it off'. When something happened that one of us didn't like, we threw popcorn at the screen, booing the character.

It was great fun and I was still laughing so hard that tears leaked from my eyes as we hit rewind and Dallas stood and danced along with Channing after it was all over. She grabbed Harper's hand, pulling her up with her and Harper joined in. Frankly, I had more fun watching them goofing around than I did watching the movie. The movie was great to watch, but I'd have rather been cuddled up with Wroth in my roost that had somehow become *our* roost. Wroth had gone out with the rest of his band—minus Liam who never went out anymore—as well as Shane and a few members of both Trance and Alchemy, but he hadn't looked all that happy about it.

In the last two weeks our relationship had gone back to almost what it had been over a year ago. We slept together every night, made love without actually having sex countless times a day. Only this time Wroth told me he loved me. Every day. Every. Day. I still had to pinch myself because it was hard to believe he had actually said those three little words to me. Wroth loved me. I'd be lying if I said I'd never thought he'd loved me. I'd always known that he did. A little at least. It had been his desire for me that I'd always questioned.

I wasn't a vain person. I looked in the mirror and knew that I was pretty. But when a sexy rocker like Wroth could have any woman he wanted, it made it a little more difficult to see my beauty. Especially when there were little Barbie dolls throwing themselves at him on a daily basis. It was why I'd felt so rejected during our last short-lived relationship when he wouldn't let me touch him. Why couldn't I touch what dozens of other women had touched without having to beg for it? Hundreds? Maybe even thousands?

Since the morning Zander had interrupted our love playing, I hadn't tried to touch Wroth below the waist no matter how hot we got, and I sure as hell hadn't begged him to let me. I didn't think I could stand his rejection this time around if he told me no or pulled away if I touched him.

"Dance with us," Harper shouted as she grabbed my hand, surprising me out of my

Wroth-filled musings, and pulled me in between herself and Dallas.

"Someone record this shit," Dallas called, rubbing herself very sexily up and down my back, making me giggle. "Axton is gonna have some serious footage to get him going tonight with these hotties sexing it up in here."

Natalie and Jenna were throwing popcorn at us instead of the screen now. I didn't know what I was doing, but I tried to go for sexy as I rubbed myself between the two beautiful women as the three of us swayed to the music. From the corner of my eyes I saw Lana recording our little show and felt my cheeks fill with pink, but didn't stop. I would send this to Wroth as soon as I could and then Axton wouldn't be the only one who had some footage to view later.

The thought of Wroth watching me dance with two incredibly beautiful women made me more daring. We were all friends here and it was just harmless fun. I grabbed Harper's hand and started sucking on her fingers, remembering his reaction to the way Dallas had done much the same thing to my own fingers so long ago. Harper made a sexy moaning sound, grinning and winking at me as I gazed up at her through my lashes.

"Damn, now that is sexy," Lana murmured from her seat on the couch. "Seriously, Marissa. You're turning me bisexual right now." She lowered her phone, shaking her head at me. "Do you think Wroth would have too big a fit if I asked you to have a threesome with me and Drake?"

From the glint in her honey-brown eyes and the grin on her face I knew she was teasing—Lana letting someone that close to Drake? Yeah, that wasn't ever going to happen. But the offer alone was enough to cause my face to turn beet red. "I'm pretty sure he would castrate your husband, Lana." Wroth had gotten very territorial in the last two weeks. Sure he was more affectionate, but his possessiveness was downright animalistic at times. Men couldn't smile at me without him turning into a rage monster.

If I said I didn't like it, it would be telling the lie of the century. I loved it. But it made me fear for the safety of the men in my life. Every man with the exception of my brother was a potential target.

A firm knock on the bus's door had us all turning as the door opened just seconds later, without anyone giving permission to whomever it was to come in. Devlin stepped into the living room, his hair pulled back into a ponytail at the base of his neck. He didn't give anyone a second glance as he narrowed his eyes on Natalie and went straight for her. She didn't say a word as he stopped in front of her. Harper and Lana gaped at him as he bent and picked Natalie up before carrying her back toward the roosts.

"That was ballsy," Jenna muttered as she threw a handful of popcorn at the rock star's back.

"Do I want to know?" Lana asked the youngest girl in the room.

"Nope." Jenna shook her head, her face impassive, letting everyone know that she wasn't about to spill her sister's secrets. "Pretend you didn't see that, Lana. It will make your life a hell of a lot easier."

"But…" Harper glanced from where Natalie had just been sitting, then down the hall to where the warped door of the sleeping area was now firmly closed behind the couple. "She… No… Right..?" She looked so confused and conflicted that it was almost adorable.

"Like I said, pretend you didn't see that. Drake and Shane really don't need to know right now." Jenna stood. "I'm going to head back to our bus. If Dev is back then the others will be soon. Shane doesn't need to be in the vicinity of this place in a few minutes."

When a moan came from the back of the bus, Harper was quick to follow the younger girl out. "Yeah, you're right. I don't need him hulking out tonight. Lana, you coming?"

"Yeah, yeah." She tried to get up but her stomach was a big obstacle. She looked up at me with a pout. "Help a bitch out, Marissa."

Laughing, I offered her both my hands and helped her to stand. "See you later." I returned her hug and walked with her to the door as the three left. "Message me that video when you get the chance."

Lana winked up at me from the bottom of the steps. "You got it, sexy."

When I turned around, it was to find Dallas had taken Lana's spot on the couch. Her gaze was on the hallway that led to the roosts. "Something's up with Natalie. Have you noticed how she's been acting lately? And it hasn't just been in the last few weeks since this tour started. Linc has hinted that her entire personality has been off for a while now." She shifted on the couch and I sat down beside her. Her concerned blue eyes looked questioningly over at me. "Have you noticed anything off?"

I grimaced. "Yes and no. I had noticed that she was quieter before the tour started, before she cut her hair. She doesn't go out with Linc like she used to, and she has seemed kind of tired lately. But..." I sighed and pushed my hair out of my face. "But I hadn't really thought about it, Dallas. I was so caught up in my own crap that I didn't pay any attention to what was going on with Natalie at the time."

She grasped my hands, giving them a reassuring squeeze. "Of course you were. Things didn't end pretty with Wroth last spring any more than they had with Dev and Nat. No one could blame you for not paying attention to what was going on with her. How are you, by the way? From an outside point of view you and Wroth seem to be closer than ever."

"I guess we are." I bit my lip, something that had become a very bad habit lately. Just the evening before, Liam had scolded me for pulling a Kristen Stewart because I was always biting my bottom lip. "Wroth told me he loves me."

One blond brow rose, but she didn't look particularly surprised. "Yeah, I've heard him say it a few times myself. He always has loved you, Rissa. He was just a pussy last spring. I never for one second believed that he meant for you to get hurt. But the real question should be, do you believe it? Do you forgive him for what he did? Do you still love him? Because even though I've heard that big scary piece of delicious man candy whispering that he loves you, I've yet to hear you return the sentiment."

I looked away. It was true. I hadn't returned the words. Hadn't even tried to utter them. I might have forgiven his slip up, his cheating, but I couldn't bring myself to tell him I loved him. Something was continuing to hold the words back. I'd given up on my side of the bet I'd made with Natalie. Had told her just the day before that I was backing out of our bet and that as soon as we got home all she had to do was tell me when she wanted to start her vacation and I would happily fulfil my side of the wager. But maybe, even though I had given up on revenge, part of me still wanted to hurt him. By not telling Wroth I loved him, I was withholding something that I could tell he was desperate to hear, to be assured of my love for him.

And. I. Just. Couldn't.

Forgiving something so destructive to a relationship such as cheating was one thing. Forgetting was something entirely different. And I was still haunted by it. The memory of seeing Wroth with some skank on her knees in front of him flashed through my mind at least once a day and each time I was left feeling shattered all over again. When that happened, I always needed to get away, to hide from everyone while I got myself back together. To fight the sudden need to erase those pictures from my mind at all costs.

Rhett was watching me closer and closer every day and I knew it was because he was scared that I was going to do something to hurt myself. But I wasn't going to do that. I'd already promised myself that no matter how depressed I got, hurting myself wasn't the answer. That didn't make Rhett feel any better and I could see his inner struggle to keep my secret to himself as his concern for my wellbeing grew.

"Rissa?"

Dallas's soft voice pulled me out of my deep thoughts and I realized I hadn't answered her yet. "I do love him, Dallas. I just… I can't seem to say the words. Every time he tells me that he loves me and I don't say the words back, I can see the pain in his eyes. It kills me to see it, but I still can't say the words out loud."

"You're still scared he's going to cheat again." I shrugged and Dallas nodded empathetically. "I can see where you're coming from, sweetie. Thinking that the man who basically owns your soul is just one step away from crushing your heart into a pile of dust is something that I've got some experience with. I thought that Axton cheated on me when we first got together…" She grimaced. "I know now that he didn't cheat, but the evidence was damning. And—"

I held up my hands, stopping her before she could say another word. "Wait. You keep talking like Wroth didn't really cheat. That it just appeared to have happened. Dallas, I saw him with that girl! I saw her on her knees right in front of him with his... And he..." I broke off, unable to say the words without completely breaking down. "He cheated, Dallas."

She gave me an unconvinced look. "You think so? You're so sure of that? He actually told you that it happened?" She shook her blond head. "Marissa, I was there during that tour. I saw how Wroth Niall was with you before everything even started. When we were at the farm, that man would go out of his way to make sure nothing hurt you. Nothing. The man even bent over backwards to try and keep everyone around you from using bad language because he knew it embarrassed you and he wanted us to respect you. He would sit and just watch cheesy old shows with you when I could tell he was bored out of his ever loving mind. But he did it all to make you happy.

"What you saw that night? I don't know what it was exactly, but I can tell you this much. Wroth would have probably killed himself before he did something that he knew would hurt you. He worships you, he always has." Dallas stood, giving me a small, grim smile. "Talk to the man, Marissa. Get his side of the story before you continue to make him pay for something he might be completely innocent of."

I couldn't speak as she turned and left the bus. Tears burned my eyes and clogged my throat. My heart was beating hard and my hands were suddenly damp. Could she be right? Had Wroth really not cheated?

CHAPTER 21

WROTH

I woke with Marissa in my arms. Her head was tucked under my chin, one arm wrapped over my waist and one knee tucked between my legs. It was the perfect way to wake up every morning. With a contented sigh I pressed a kiss to the top of her head and tried to stretch as much as possible without waking her. I was tired after the last three days of concerts.

There had been no break during the days since we'd had morning interviews at six fucking o'clock for local radio stations, followed by all-day events that drained me more than being under the hot lights on stage performing for more than an hour. Then as soon as one show was finished it was back on the road and starting the whole thing all over again in the next city. And during the last three days, I'd barely seen Marissa for five minutes during the day.

If I hadn't had her to fall asleep with every night, I probably would have gone insane by now.

Marissa sighed in her sleep and cuddled closer against me, her lips brushing over my chest as she kissed me in her sleep. "Mm."

I tightened my hold on her, afraid she would move away in her sleep if I didn't.

From the roost across from ours I heard a soft moan and realized that I wasn't the only one awake. It was all too obvious that Devlin and Natalie were wide awake in Devlin's roost at the moment. When Natalie moaned a little louder followed by Devlin's curse, Marissa's eyes opened and her face twisted in grimace. "Again? Didn't we fall asleep to them last night?" she muttered sleepily.

I leaned down to kiss her lips. "Yup." But the sounds those two had been making had gotten us both worked up and I'd taken my time getting my girl to heaven before we'd fallen asleep in each other's arms to the sounds of the other couple still going at it. Devlin and I both seriously needed to look into getting our own buses, and soon. I reached for Marissa's hand and brought it to my lips, kissing her fingertips one by one. "What do you say we give them a run for their money in a nosiest love-making contest?" I suggested.

Pink filled her cheeks but she grinned up at me. "I like that idea," she murmured so softly it was like a caress down my spine.

With a happy growl, I pulled her over me and kissed her long and deep. Marissa was still naked from where I'd undressed us both the night before and the feel of her hot, soaking wet pussy brushing over my throbbing cock was enough to force a groan from me. I gripped her ass and spread her thighs wider so that the head of my cock would fit perfectly against her clit. She ground her hips down against me, making me see bright spots behind my closed lids from the sheer pleasure of her heat grinding on my agonizing flesh.

When I thrust the tips of two fingers into her opening from behind, she broke our hungry kiss to let a wanton little moan escape. She felt so good, so tight and wet and scalding hot. I wanted to sink my dick deep inside of her until we were completely one, but I'd somehow kept sane enough over the last several weeks to keep from taking her virginity. It was killing me, but I would suffer the fires of hell if I had to. I wasn't taking Marissa's virginity until my ring was on her finger and she was Mrs. Wroth Niall.

It might seem archaic, and if the tabloid trash mags ever got hold of that little bit of information they would have a field day. But I was an old-fashioned kind of guy. I loved this girl with everything inside of me and was going to make sure that we did this the right way, just like my mother would have wanted me to do if she had still been alive. Marissa was so innocent and pure and she deserved to still be that way on her wedding day.

Of course I still had to ask her. I hadn't yet because I had special plans for asking her something so fucking important. It was what I'd asked Emmie to help me with and our stop in Kansas was just the next day. I was excited to ask her to spend the rest of her life with me, and at the same time I was terrified. I was scared out of my mind that she was going to turn me down.

In the last few weeks, I'd told my girl that I loved her whenever the words would whisper through my conscious. Which was a lot. But there hadn't been one time when she had repeated them. I was okay with that, at least I kept telling myself I was okay with it. The pain that would slice through me with the absence of her words of love was like a chainsaw slicing me in half.

I couldn't understand why she never told me she loved me when I could see what she felt for me shining back at me in her eyes every time I looked at her. Even now, as she moaned my name and dripped her release on my quivering dick I could see how much she loved me. "Wroth!"

"That's it, sweetheart. Come for me," I encouraged as I gripped her ass cheeks harder, grinding her pussy against me until she convulsed with her orgasm.

With a loud cry she fell against my chest, her breaths coming in hard pants as she slowly came down from the high of her release. When she lifted her head and smiled at me I turned us onto our sides. My dick was still rock hard and my balls were tight, ready to spill my own release. "Touch me, Mari," I commanded.

The smile on her face dimmed and she pulled her hand back when I reached for it. I grimaced, knowing that she was remembering all those times I'd refused to let her touch me last spring. I hadn't realized at the time how much damage I'd been doing to her pride. She hadn't made the same pleas to touch me in the last few weeks, had never touched me below my navel during our love play sessions. If she had, I would have gladly let her take her time exploring every inch of my body if that was what she wanted to do to me. She hadn't though, and I hadn't let myself think about it much, but I could see now that my refusing to let her touch me then was affecting us now.

I caught her hand and lifted it to my mouth once again. I trapped and held her gaze as I kissed her open palm. "I love you, sweetheart." I watched the muscles work in her throat as she swallowed hard and tried to hide my pain when she didn't so much as open her mouth. "Listen to me for a minute, Mari. Okay?" After only a small hesitation she nodded. "Before…back then? I couldn't let you touch me. I wanted you so badly that if I let you touch me I wouldn't have been able to contain myself. I wouldn't have been able to keep from sinking deep into your beautiful body and making love to you like I wanted to so badly back then—like I want to do right now. I still have trouble controlling my need to be inside of you, sweetheart."

Tears filled her eyes and she lowered her gaze to my chest. "Why won't you? I want you to make love to me like that, Wroth. I need you to make love to me like that."

"Because I want your husband to take your virginity," I muttered. "He's the only one who should ever take that from you. Do you understand?"

Blue eyes widened and she gasped. "What?"

I cupped her face, fighting back my smile at her outraged expression. "He will be a very lucky man, Marissa."

"So you won't make love to me?" she demanded, suddenly sounding angry. "Because I'm a virgin? For real?" She pulled away from me and I realized that she wasn't just angry but pissed the fuck off. She moved farther away from me, wrapping the sheet around her gorgeous body as she climbed down from the roost. "You are such a fucking asshole."

I quickly reached for my boxers at the end of the bed and pulled them on as I followed her out of the sleeping area and down the hall to the living room. Thankfully no one else was up, or if they were then they were off the bus since we had arrived at our next stop hours ago. The living room was empty and she tied the sheet tighter around her chest before turning to face me. "Marissa—"

"I can't believe you. I really can't." She pushed her hair out of her face with a hand that trembled. "You said you loved me, and then tell me you won't have sex with me. Because you want me to be a damn virgin for my husband? Yet, you will let complete strangers blow you?

And I know you had sex with *her*. Why else wouldn't you have come back to the hotel that night?"

How had we gone from making love, to arguing about her getting married, to this? I thought she had forgiven me for that night. Thought that it was behind us, even though I'd wanted to explain it to her. Yet she had refused every time I'd brought it up.

Well, no fucking more.

"I didn't have sex with her!" I couldn't help but roar when I saw the tears that had filled her eyes. Her tears should come with a damn warning label. At the sight of Marissa Bryant's tears your insides will wilt and die.

For weeks now she had refused to let me explain about that fucking night with the groupie. But I couldn't let her keep thinking that I had cheated on her. "And she sure as hell didn't give me a blow job. You only saw, what? Five seconds? If you had waited five more you would have seen me push that stupid slut off me."

"Yeah right," Marissa said with a snort of disbelief. "She was on her knees, Wroth. And your pants were unbuttoned."

"Unbuttoned maybe, but not down." I raked my hands through my hair, silently begging one of Emmie's fucking gods to help me here. My fucking life depending on this girl believing me right now. "I was checking on my Fenders, making sure that Pock had put them where they were supposed to be, and she caught me by surprise. One minute she was in front of me rambling some drunken gibberish, and the next she was on her knees with her hands on the zipper of my jeans. She was drunk and I didn't know how to get her off me without hurting her. But when she nearly got my dick out, I pushed her off. I didn't care if she got hurt or not. I just didn't want her to touch me. She ended up on her ass, crying because she was drunk and mad since I'd turned her down earlier that night." When Marissa still looked like she didn't believe me I started to get mad too. "It's true. I didn't cheat on you."

"Then where were you all night?" she demanded, more tears spilling from her eyes in a faster stream. The sight of those tears gutted me, but I wasn't going to let them distract me from this conversation. This was too important not to get it out in the open. My future with her hinged on it. "Why didn't you come back to the hotel room that night?"

"I took her home." I told her and she turned away from me, shaking her head and laughing humorlessly in skepticism. "Pock and I took her home. She'd twisted her ankle when she fell and she was so drunk she didn't make much sense. So I got Pock to help me take her home. When we got to her house, there was a big party going on that her roommates were throwing and Pock wanted to stay. I left him there and went back to the hotel, but by then Dev and Z had already gotten into a fight. I spent the rest of the night with Zander in a coffee shop letting him bitch about Devlin and Natalie."

Marissa still had her back to me, but I saw the way her shoulders dropped a little and prayed that she was starting to believe me. I'd wanted to own up to what had happened that night for more than a year now, should have done it the night when she had thrown me out of her life. I'd thought, however, that she would cool down and realize that I would never have cheated on her. Never. She meant too much to me to throw away what we had with some meaningless fuck with a stranger.

Yeah, I'll admit that I'd felt guilty for what had happened that night because for one insane second, when that drunken girl had had her hands on my zipper, I'd thought about letting her suck my dick. It would have proven to myself that I really didn't deserve Marissa. That I wasn't a good enough man for her. That one, stupid moment of insanity had made me think I deserved for her to hate me for a long, long time. But now that I had forgiven myself and had her forgiveness for my past, I knew that not only was she made for me but I was the only man who would ever cherish her the way she deserved.

No one would ever love Marissa Bryant as much as I did.

CHAPTER 22

MARISSA

The blood rushing through my ears made it impossible to hear anything over the beating of my heart. I clutched the sheet tighter to my chest, the tears on my face drying as Wroth's words repeated over and over again in my head.

For days now I'd been thinking about what Dallas had said, that she hadn't thought that Wroth had really cheated. She knew that he loved me too much to even think about it. I'd been living in denial, trying to convince myself that it had happened, when I knew deep down that what she said was the truth. Maybe he hadn't said the words back then, but I had known that Wroth loved me. He was a man who wasn't gentle by nature, yet he'd always been so with me.

All my life he had cherished me in one way or another. Whether it was joining the marines so that his parents wouldn't lose their farm and so that I could still live with them, or helping my brother pay for my medical treatments and standing by that damned window every day that I'd been in isolation, or holding onto his control and not taking something he thought himself undeserving of. He always made sure that no matter what, I was taken care of.

In the past half hour, as I'd gone from having one of the best orgasms in my life to hearing him tell me he wouldn't take what I so desperately wanted to give him—that my virginity was for my future husband—I'd let my anger overwhelm me and I'd lost my temper with him for only the second time in my life. All because I'd wanted him to say he wanted to be my husband.

And for the first time in all the years that I'd known and loved Wroth Niall, he had lost his temper with me. I'd never heard him speak louder than a soft roar in my vicinity but just now he had yelled so loud I was surprised that the glass in the windows hadn't shattered. It was what I needed though, his angry words shouted at me as he admitted what had really happened that night was all the proof I needed that what he was saying was the truth.

I suddenly felt very, very stupid, however. I should have known that Wroth wouldn't do something like that to me. I should have had more trust in his feelings for me, even though he hadn't said the words to me then. Wroth wasn't like other guys out there who would jump at any chance to get between some girl's thighs. He loved me and respected me far too much to ever do that.

"Marissa?" Wroth's voice was calmer now, but rougher than I'd ever heard it. "Please, sweetheart. Say something." His voice cracked.

I scrubbed the last of my tears away and slowly turned to face him. "I believe you."

He seemed to relax a little as he held out his hands to me. "You do? If you don't I can get Emmie to find that chick somehow and make her tell you the truth. Or Pock will tell you. He was there."

I shook my head. "No, no I don't need her or Pock to tell me anything. I believe you, Wroth. I think deep down I knew that you wouldn't do something like that to me. You loved me then too, didn't you?"

He wrapped his arms around my waist and buried his face in my hair. "Yes, sweetheart. I've loved you for most of my life. You have no idea how much, could never understand how deep my love for you goes."

A small smile lifted the corners of my mouth as I held onto him even tighter. "Oh, I'm pretty sure I can understand it better than you think." I turned my head and kissed the side of his face. "I love you, Wroth," I whispered.

The big man in my arms went completely still. I heard his inhale and when it wasn't automatically exhaled, I pulled back, concerned. When I saw the glint in his espresso eyes, my own breath caught in my chest. "S-say it again, Mari."

"I love you, Wroth. More than you will ever know." Strong arms lifted me up until I was at his eye level.

His gaze ate up the sight of me before he shook his head and pulled me forcefully against his hard body. "I love you too, Marissa. You are my world, girl. Nothing matters to me except for you. Do you understand that? Only you."

"I—"

The door of the bus opened so suddenly that the door made a squeaking protest as it swung back and slammed into the outside of the bus. Wroth's hold on me tightened painfully as Liam rushed into the living room. His eyes were wild, his breathing coming in sharp pants as his eyes raked over me. "Are you okay? One of the roadies was walking by and heard you screaming and crying." His gaze went to Wroth. "He said that you were shouting at her. What the fuck have you done this time, motherfucker?"

"Don't talk like that in front of your sister," Wroth gritted out.

"You make my sister cry and the first words out of your fu…freakin' mouth is for me not to cuss in front of her?" Liam's nostrils flared. "I will kill you if you hurt her again, Wroth. I don't care if I did give you permiss—"

"I'm not going to hurt her, damn it," Wroth roared, cutting whatever my brother had been about to say off. "And if you would get the hell out of here, we could get back to making up like we should have done last spring."

Liam's mouth snapped closed and he glanced from his cousin to me, taking in how I was dressed. Blushing, I wrapped the sheet closer around me and bit my bottom lip. "Will you please stop biting that damned lip, Rissa? It's annoying as hell."

I released my bottom lip with a laugh and was happy to see that Liam's anger was fading away. He looked back at Wroth, a small smile tilting his lips upward. "So everything's okay in here? You didn't break my sister's heart again?"

"Everything is great in here at the moment," I told my brother before Wroth could open his mouth. "And no, Wroth didn't break my heart again, Li. If anything he just put it back together again."

Liam let out a relieved sigh. "Good. Good." Slowly he backed away. "Well, then. I'll just go so that you two can get back to... whatever it was... I really don't want to see the images that're already forming in my head of how you two are going to make up..." He grimaced. "I'm glad you're okay, Ris. I love you."

"I love you too, Li," I called after him as the door slammed shut behind him.

As soon as my brother was gone, Wroth was pulling me back into his arms. Espresso eyes were glittering down at me with a mixture of amusement, love, and need. "I love you, Marissa. Then, now, forever."

I soaked in those words. Right then, in that very moment, I had never been happier. "I love you more."

Wroth growled low in his throat and lifted me off my feet. Instinctively I wrapped my legs around his waist, gasping when I felt his hardened flesh flex against my core through the sheet. "Sweetheart, that just isn't possible."

"Oh yeah?" I teased as I brushed my lips over his. "Prove it."

With a deep, rumbly laugh, he walked with me still in his arms back toward the sleeping compartments. The sounds coming from the roost across from ours was still hot and passionate and I rolled my eyes up at Wroth. "Animals," he said with disgust, making me giggle. "Get ready to scream for me, Mari."

My sex flooded with liquid heat and I scooted across our bed, holding my arms open for him as he climbed in and closed the curtain. "Does this mean you're going to really make love to me?" I asked shyly.

"It means I'm going to lick your pussy until you come all over my face and then you're going to use this gorgeous mouth on me." He rubbed his thumb over my bottom lip. "The love making will come soon, sweetheart. Very, very soon."

CHAPTER 23

MARISSA

I felt like I was floating on a cloud the rest of that day and well into the next. I didn't know how it was possible to be as happy as I was right then, but I hoped the feeling never went away.

On the second day in Kansas, I woke up with a tray of breakfast being placed on the mattress in our roost. I stretched and smiled as I picked up the little note on the tray that had a covered dish of something yummy smelling, a small glass of orange juice, my daily dose of Synthroid that I would have to take for the rest of my life because of my underactive thyroid, and a small little vase with a single flower in it.

A poppy! My obsession with *The Wizard of Oz* made recognizing the little flower easy. It was also one of my favorite flowers and Wroth knew it.

I grinned as I read the note written in Wroth's disaster he called handwriting. Luckily I had years of practice deciphering it.

> *Enjoy your breakfast sweetheart. When you're done, take a shower and put on the outfit Natalie left hanging for you in the bathroom. Someone will be waiting to bring you to me in two hours. I love you so much Marissa. Then. Now. Forever. –Wroth.*

My heart melted at his note, and then curiosity and excitement kicked in. Wroth had told me last night before we'd fallen asleep in each other's arms that he had something important to do this morning and when he was done I could meet up with him and spend the afternoon sightseeing with him. All he'd had to say was Oz Museum and I'd been hooked.

My excitement got the better of me and I rushed through my breakfast, delighted that it was my favorite with a Colorado omelet with salsa and toast. I knew that Wroth hadn't made this for me because he couldn't even boil an egg let alone make an omelet. This had Linc written all over it, but it was still incredibly adorable.

After I was finished I showered, noticing as I stepped into the large tiled walk-in shower that there was a zipped up dress bag hanging from the back of the bathroom door. I wanted to open it and see what Natalie had picked out for me to wear, wondering briefly why she would even need to pick out my clothes, but decided to wait until I was washed before peeking.

I took my time showering, shampooing and conditioning my hair before shaving everything that needed some attention. Unlike the majority of my girlfriends, I didn't like getting waxed. Call me a cry baby all you want, but that crap hurt. I'd gone through plenty of physical pain. I didn't want to willingly put myself through it ever again.

When the water grew tepid I turned it off and dried myself before climbing out. Since today was special and I would be taking all kinds of pictures at the Oz Museum, I was going to look my best. I blew my hair dry then curled the ends before putting on a little makeup—just a little foundation, some eye shadow and mascara, with gloss completing it.

Finally, I let myself open the dress bag and nearly fell on my ass when I stumbled back in surprise. No. Freaking. Way. My heart moved up to my throat, making it impossible to breathe as I lifted a trembling hand to touch the ruby red shoes that were hanging with the simple white sundress. Tears fell from my eyes, ruining the makeup I'd just applied.

When I picked up the shoes, a piece of paper fell to the floor and I carefully bent to pick it up. Like the note that had been on my breakfast tray, it was written in Wroth's handwriting.

'A heart is not judged by how much you love, but by how much you are loved by others.' You are loved more

than you will ever know, Marissa. By our friends, and your brother but especially by me. –Wroth

The famous quote that the Wizard had told the Tin Man from *The Wizard of Oz* brought even more tears to my eyes. It took me forever to get my tears under control and by the time I'd fixed my makeup and dressed, the two hours Wroth had given me to be ready by had been over by a good twenty minutes.

Cursing, I slipped the ruby heels on as I rushed through the bus. When I opened a door, an older man with graying hair dressed in a chauffeur's suit stood just a few feet away. He had a sign in his hand with my name on it. His eyes went to my shoes and grinned. "Miss Bryant?"

I nodded. "Yes, that's me."

"I thought it might be." He took off his hat and offered me his arm. "This way, please."

Excitement filled me once more and I took his arm, feeling surprisingly safe with the older man. We walked through the deserted parking lot, something that surprised me the most. I'd known that the bus was empty but where was everyone else? I didn't even see the roadies, just a few security guards that I didn't recognize.

The chauffeur placed me in the back of a black limo and moments later pulled out into traffic. The partition was left down and he talked to me as he drove. And drove. And drove. He kept driving for over an hour before he stopped right outside the biggest warehouse I'd ever seen.

The parking lot only had a few vans parked around the side of the warehouse but other than that the place looked deserted.

Nervous now, I hesitated before getting out of the limo when the chauffeur, who had told me his name was Larry, opened the door and offered me his hand. Seeing my reluctance, Larry smiled encouragingly. "I promise that this is where you want to be, Miss Bryant. Mrs. Armstrong made sure I knew exactly where I was going this morning."

I relaxed a little when he mentioned Emmie and finally took his hand, letting him help me out of the limo. Once I was out, I gazed up at the warehouse. It was even bigger than I had originally thought. From the outsides I could imagine the inside being big enough to hold two or three football fields. Why in the world would Emmie want me to come here? Why would Wroth?

With my hand on his arm, Larry escorted me to the side door of the warehouse and knocked twice. I frowned up at the blue sky as we waited until the door opened. When it did, I nearly screamed.

"Welcome to Oz, Marissa."

I gaped at Emmie as she grinned and stepped back, letting me into the wonderland that the warehouse had been turned into. Fresh tears blurred my vision and I hurriedly blinked them back so that I could see what was in front of me.

Oh. My. Gosh. I'd just stepped into Oz. With a happy little twirl, I took everything around me in. There were trees, poppies, and… and… a freaking yellow brick road! I looked back at Emmie, convinced that I was dreaming.

"What's going on, Emmie?" I demanded.

Emmie shrugged. "Someone wanted to give you your dream. And with a little help from everyone who loves you, and the Oz Museum, I was able to make it happen." She stepped back and lifted a finger to her lips. "Shh. Do you hear that?" I frowned, not hearing anything. "Munchkins."

It seemed like they suddenly appeared out of nowhere because I was suddenly surrounded by munchkins. Children in various ages all dressed up like the little people from my favorite movie. They all surrounded me and hugged me. A laugh bubbled up and I was unable to contain it as I hugged the kids back.

"Munchkins, munchkins!" a voice I knew well called out and when I looked around, I spotted Dallas, dressed up as Glinda the Good Witch. I had to press my lips together as I saw the tattooed blonde bombshell dressed up like Glinda in full costume—right down to the wings and wand.

The children around me drew back, making room for Dallas the Good Witch. When I glanced back to ask Emmie if this was for real, she was gone. Dallas tapping me on the nose with her wand forced me to turn my attention back to her and once again it was nearly impossible to keep from giggling at the sight of her dressed like this.

"How much did Emmie have to pay you to wear that?" I asked with a grin.

Dallas shook her head at me. "All she had to say was that this was for you. I—we..."—she nodded around her at everything— "...did this because we love you." She cleared her throat. "Now listen up, Marissa Bryant. What you seek is at the end of the yellow brick road." I giggled and she rolled her blue eyes at me. "Stop it. I'm trying to be serious."

"Sorry," I murmured, trying to keep my giggles from overcoming me.

"As you should be, bitch." The munchkins all gasped at her use of a bad word and Dallas sighed loudly. "Where was I? Oh, yeah. What you seek is at the end of the yellow brick road, inside the gates of Emerald City. Along the way, you will run into friends who love you as much as I do. Each has something special for you that will make your decision easier to make."

"My decision?" I couldn't help but catch that odd choice of words.

Dallas tapped me on the nose again with her wand. "When a man loves you this much, Marissa, I don't think it would be much of a decision to make." She winked and stepped back. "Okay, munchkins. She must be on her way. He won't like having to wait longer than he needs to."

"Who won't?" I demanded. "Wroth?"

Of course Dallas didn't tell me whether it was or not. I just got another wink and then the sudden sound of a violin playing "Follow the

Yellow Brick Road" filled the air. For real? This was really happening? I wasn't in some kind of weird dream, was I?

"Follow the yellow brick road, Marissa," Dallas commanded.

I stepped back. "Okay, then." Grinning, I rolled my eyes at her and stepped onto the yellow brick road's path.

One of the munchkins stepped forward and I was startled when I realized it was Lucy. "Follow the yellow brick road!"

"Lucy!" I hugged her.

Another munchkin stepped forward. "Follow the yellow brick road!"

"Mia!" I bent to kiss her cheek and she giggled but stepped back before I could hug her.

"Follow the yellow brick road!" the munchkins said in chorus.

"I am," I told them. "See? I'm following the yellow brick road."

"Good luck," Dallas called after me and I waved before doing as I'd been so forcefully instructed to do.

Giggling like a child, I walked down the yellow path, passing the spot where the Scarecrow would have been with a nostalgic smile before continuing. A little farther and I saw a statue of the Tin Man and stopped for a moment to check it out.

Honestly, I'd seen better statues of Tin Man, but it was the thought that counted. I stepped closer, raising my fist to knock on his chest to see if he would sound hollow or not when a hand shot out and grabbed me. I screamed and stepped back, but Tin Man had a tight hold on my wrist.

"Not so fast there, Dorothy."

My fear instantly faded and I glared up at my brother. "You scared me to death."

Liam grinned down at me, the silver paint on his face cracking just a little at the corners of his mouth. "Sorry, Ris."

My eyes trailed over him from top to bottom and, unlike when I'd seen Dallas as Glinda, I couldn't contain my giggles at seeing my big bad brother dressed up like the Tin Man. "I can't believe you would dress up like this for me."

His eyes darkened. "Believe it. I love you so much, Rissa. You are the most important person in my life. I would die for you." Strong arms wrapped around me in a hug and I got to experience my first Tin Man hug ever, made all the better because it was one of the two men that I loved the most in the world. Stepping back, I was surprised when I saw the tears in my brother's eyes that he was trying to hide. "All I've ever wanted for you was your happiness, Rissa. And if my dressing up like a freakin' can of sardines will bring that smile to your face, I'd do it again and again."

"Li..." I blinked back my tears, a sob choking me as I tried to hold it back. "I love you to, Li."

He cleared his throat and offered me his arm, just as a violin started playing "We're Off to See the Wizard". "That's my cue," Liam informed me with a smile. "Shall we go see the wizard, Ris?"

"With you? I'd love to, brother mine."

"I'm not skipping," Liam muttered as we stepped back onto the yellow path.

"Agreed." I giggled.

Onward we walked, and I tried not to skip as the music continued to fill the air. This was quite possibly the most fun I'd ever had in my life. The only thing that would have made it better was if Wroth were there with me, but he was in Emerald City waiting for me. It couldn't have been anyone else, because Wroth was the only person I was 'seeking' as Dallas the Good Witch had said.

When the music faded and Liam stopped, I nearly pouted. I was having fun, so why did we have to stop? "Li-"

"Shh." He covered my mouth. "Listen, Ris."

I frowned and glanced around, not hearing anything out of the ordinary. "What? I don't hear…" The rumble that came from a bush just a few feet away made me jump and Liam stepped in front of me to protect me.

"Come out of there," Liam demanded. The bush shook and the rumble came again. Liam took a step closer to the bush and we both jumped back when a man in Lion's costume popped his head up and then stood.

"Gotcha," Axton said and chuckled as he stepped out of the bush. "Dude, you were supposed to be expecting it. Why'd you jump too?"

Liam laughed, shaking his head. "Just in the moment, man."

I rushed forward, hugging Axton as I took in his costume. "I never imagined Lion and Glinda the Good Witch as a couple before."

"Glinda's pretty hot, huh?" He hugged me back and kissed me, tickling my cheek with his furry face. The violin started up once more and Axton offered me his arm. "Shall we?"

I was going to giggle myself to death before the day was over, I realized as I took Axton's arm and then my brother's and we continued on our way toward the gates of Emerald City in the distance. The yellow brick road wound round and round, making the walk toward the city a long one as we passed actors on wires dressed up as flying monkeys.

As we rounded a corner that was full of tall, fake trees, a witch's cackle had my head snapping up and the Wicked Witch stepped forward. Honestly I'd never seen a more beautiful Wicked Witch. Or a more pregnant one. With green makeup on and a black dress stretched tight over her pregnant belly, Lana was the perfect Wicked Witch.

"Give me your shoes, bitch," she commanded as she stepped forward to kiss my cheek. "No, seriously. Those are to die for. Hand them over."

"No way," I said and laughed. "You're such a shoe whore. These are mine."

"Damn. Okay then. It's not like I could wear them right now anyway. I'd fall and break my neck with this belly keeping me so off balance."

She glanced from Axton to Liam, grinning. "Nice."

Liam gave her a once over, whistling his own appreciation. "Back at ya, gorgeous. But don't tell Drake I said that."

When the music started again, Lana clapped her hands together. "Okay, let's go. It's not much farther now." She linked her arm through mine and we walked ahead of the men as we drew closer to the gates of Emerald City.

As we neared the gates, a Green Guard stepped forward and kissed the Wicked Witch. "I heard you cackling and it was the sexiest sound I've ever heard, Angel."

Axton and Liam snickered behind me and I turned to shush them. "Stop it," I hissed at them.

When Drake raised his head, he glared at his two friends before that blue-gray gaze landed on me and softened. "Someone's been getting anxious, Rissa." He stepped back and opened the latch on the gate. "Better go find him."

I didn't need to know who the 'him' was that Drake was talking about. No one but one man would have ever thought to give me this experience and I couldn't wait to tell him how much I loved him. I rushed past Drake and into Emerald city and stopped in my tracks at the sight before me.

Oh, Wroth…

CHAPTER 24

WROTH

At the sound of the door opening, everything inside of me tightened. This was it. There was no going back now. The next few minutes would be the defining moment in my life. Would I spend the rest of my life with the woman I needed more than I needed air to breathe… or would she walk away?

I didn't know what her answer was going to be, and the not knowing was making me shake.

Nervously, I tugged at the collar of my flannel shirt. There were pieces of straw sticking out from all angles, making me itch, which didn't make my anxiousness any easier to deal with. With a groan I glanced down at the getup I'd put on just a little while ago. I'd refused to put a sack on my head to make the Scarecrow costume more believable. Hell, Emmie was able to give Marissa the entire Oz experience. She knew how much I loved her, so she would understand if I didn't try to smother myself with a damned potato sack.

Around me, the rest of our friends sat around the arbor that Emmie and the Oz Museum had set up, all of them dressed up as a character from the movie. The munchkins were all sitting up front with their drama teacher in her own costume seated beside Dallas in her bulky Glinda the Good Witch outfit. The Demon's Wings guys were all Green Guards and everyone else was dressed as Emerald City citizens. Yeah, this was as close to perfect as Emmie had been able to get and it was pretty fucking awesome if you asked me.

And cheesy. So damned cheesy. But it was going to make my girl happy and I would do anything to make her smile. Even dress up like a fucking Scarecrow.

The door opened and in walked the most beautiful sight I'd ever laid eyes on. Marissa was breathtaking in the simple white sundress and those killer glittery ruby heels. Her makeup was smeared a little, telling me she had been crying but the look in those blue eyes told me that they had been happy tears. I breathed a small breath of relief when I saw the beaming smile on that face that I loved so much.

Behind her an alluring Wicked Witch followed by a Green Guard, Tin Man, and Lion stepped through the door and I couldn't help but grin at my friends and bandmates as they nodded their heads in greeting before taking the empty seats behind me. That just left me standing there, staring down at the girl who had the power to destroy me with one word in the next few minutes.

Her arms wrapped around me as soon as she reached me and my own went around her as I held her against me. The scent of her hair invaded my senses and I let it calm me as I tried to find the words I'd silently been rehearsing for days now.

With a soft laugh, Marissa leaned back. "I don't know how you did this, but thank you. I'd thought that we were just going to go see the museum. And you gave me *this*." Tears sparkled in her eyes and she blinked to keep them from spilling. "Thank you so much, Wroth. This means the world to me."

I swallowed hard, trying to get the words— any words—out through the lump in my throat. "You are *my* world, Marissa. I would give you this and anything else you want." I stepped back and pulled out the box that had been practically burning a hole in my pocket for over a month. When I dropped to one knee, Marissa gasped, her hands covering her mouth as the tears she'd been trying to keep at bay just seconds ago spilled free.

"I love you, Marissa. Then. Now. Forever. I gave you Oz, but all I want in return is you. Will you marry me, sweetheart?"

A sob escaped her and she shook her head, tears spilling faster. "I… You…" She shook her head harder and my stomach churned as I feared she was going to turn me down. No, no. I couldn't possibly survive if she said no.

"Wroth…" She cleared her throat, swallowed hard, and I tried to hold my own tears back as I prepared for her to turn me down. "Of course I'll marry you. I love you. Then. Now. Forever."

I closed my eyes as relief washed over me, but a tear escaped anyway and I buried my face in her dress as I wrapped my arms around her waist and thanked whoever had sent this precious girl to me so that I could love and cherish her for the rest of my life. Soft fingers combed through my hair, holding me against her as my shoulders shook and I let the tears continue to fall. She was mine. Thank God, she was mine.

Behind me there came the shouts and sudden applause as our friends and family, rockers, roadies, and actors all congratulated us. It was a long while before I lifted my head though. When I did, it was to find Marissa smiling that one smile that I would have paid any price to have perfected on canvas so that I could have that sight forever. "Hi," she whispered.

I cleared my throat. "Hey." My eyes drifted closed as she wiped my tears away with the soft pad of her thumb. "Did you really say yes?" I asked, needing to make sure I hadn't dreamed her answer.

She giggled. "Yes, I said yes. I love you, silly man. There was no other answer I could have given you."

"When?"

"When will I marry you?" I nodded. "As soon as you want."

Another breath of relief left me and I stood up, finally putting the ring on her finger. She didn't even glance down at it, her blue eyes were glued to mine and I bent to brush a kiss over her soft lips. I'd sweated bullets over what ring to pick out for her, and she didn't even care what it looked like. Damn, I loved this woman. "Now?" I breathed.

"Now what?" she asked, sounding dazed as I brushed my lips over hers again.

"Will you marry me now? Right now?" She gasped and took a step back, her eyes demanding to know if I was serious without her having to ask the question. "I told you a few days ago, Mari. The only man who will be taking your virginity is your husband. I meant that."

"But... there are things that we need to do. Like find a minister and get the license and..." She broke off. "I'm sure there are other things that we would have to do. We couldn't possibly..."

I grinned down at her and glanced over my shoulder to where Emmie and Natalie were standing with their clipboards in hands. Emmie nodded her head to the side and I saw a man in a suit step forward. Marissa followed my gaze first to Emmie and Natalie and then to the minister who pulled a Bible out of his suit jacket pocket.

Marissa snorted. "Of course we can get married today." She rolled her eyes and laughed. "Okay then. Let's get married."

CHAPTER 25

Marissa

I had to be dreaming. There just wasn't any other explanation for how happy I was or for how fast everything was moving.

As Emmie snapped the last of the buttons on the wedding dress that she had had ordered for me, I pinched my cheek. When a shot of pain flash through me, I shook my head. "I still don't believe it."

In front of me, Layla, Lana, Dallas, and Harper gave me knowing grins. "Sweetie, it doesn't matter how long you wait to get married once that ring is on your finger," Layla informed me as she glanced down at the rings on her left hand. "When it's the man you've waited your entire life for, it's going to feel like a dream regardless if you wait an hour or a year."

"But what about a honeymoon?" I asked and then blushed when I got another round of knowing smirks from my friends.

"Wroth can't leave the tour right now for a honeymoon," Emmie told me as she got the last button into place and came around to face me. "But he did ask me to get you guys your own bus. It'll be waiting for you when you meet up with us in a few days. Tonight and tomorrow night you guys will be in the honeymoon suite at the Hilton."

"But…"

"Drake will fill in for Wroth tomorrow night," Lana assured me as she smoothed something through my hair and then placed a tiara on top of my head. "There. Perfect."

"But…"

Dallas stepped forward and took my hands. Thankfully the Glinda costume was now gone because I doubted I would have been able to take her seriously if she were still wearing it. "No more buts, Rissa. You're getting married, girl. There isn't anything else to worry about but going out there and starting the rest of your life with the man who has proved above and beyond how much he adores you."

I sucked in a deep breath in hopes of keeping my sudden tears at bay. "Okay. You're right. This is really happening. Oh. Damn." I fanned my hands in front of my eyes, trying not to ruin the makeup that Dallas and Layla had just applied for me. "I don't want to cry again."

The other women laughed and then one by one kissed my cheek. "It's show time," Emmie told me as she stepped back and opened the door to the make-shift dressing room everyone had used earlier in the day to get ready for my *Wizard of Oz* experience.

When the door opened, my brother, now free of his Tin Man outfit and paint free, stood there waiting for us in a tux. When he saw me, his eyes began to glimmer with what couldn't have been mistaken for anything but tears. I walked into the arms he opened and hugged Liam. "You look good," I told him.

"You look beautiful," he said and pressed a kiss to my brow and offered me his arm just as he had earlier. Only this time we both knew he was leading me off for the last time. I was getting married. I was really getting married.

With more tears threatening to spill from my aching eyes, we followed the others out to the gates of Emerald City. With a smile the five women stepped through the door, leaving Liam and me alone until our cue. A cue no one had bothered to explain to listen for. I shook my head, hoping that Liam would know what to expect.

"I'm really happy for you, Rissa. I know that Wroth has always been the one for you and I'm glad that you two are going to spend the rest of your lives together." He smiled down at me a little sadly. "But no matter what, you will always be my little sister. Okay? If you need anything, you only have to say the word and it's yours."

"Thanks, Li. But right now I have everything I will ever want or need."

He nodded. "Yeah, Ris. I know." The first strings of violin had his head snapping up and he gave a small grimace before reaching for the door to the gate. "That's us."

We walked through the door and I saw that the chairs had been rearranged in front of the arbor so that I now had an aisle to walk up. As we got to the back of the aisle, Liam stopped and my favorite song softly filled the air. I frowned when I saw the little Italian rocker standing just off to the side of the arbor singing "Somewhere Over the Rainbow." I chanced a glance at Liam and he just shook his head.

"She was the perfect person to sing this song for you, Ris. Even Emmie knew that. Which was why she made the call." I opened my mouth to ask him how he felt about this, but he shook his head again. "This is your day, Rissa. Whatever makes it perfect is all that matters to me."

"All I needed to make this perfect was for Wroth to be the one waiting with the minister and you giving me away. The rest is immaterial." I leaned on tiptoes to kiss his cheek, having taken off the heels and replacing them with slippers instead. "But thank you, Li."

My brother cleared his throat, as if he were choked up, tightened his hold on my hand as he tucked it under his arm and took that first step that lead to my future. Finally, I let my gaze go to Wroth and my next breath got trapped in my throat as I took in the man who was about to become my husband. He wasn't wearing a tux, but his formal marines uniform. It had been years since I'd seen him wear that uniform but it still had the power to make me breathless from just looking at him.

It took every ounce of willpower I still possessed to keep from rushing up the aisle and throwing myself into his arms. His smile told me that he was having the same problem.

CHAPTER 26

WROTH

I couldn't speak. The words that I was supposed to repeat were lodged in my throat and refused to come out. Oh fuck. Oh. Fuck. I swallowed hard, trying to get through the lump that had clogged my throat the moment I'd seen Marissa standing at the end of the aisle in her wedding dress with her brother standing beside her.

There had never been a more beautiful sight than my girl standing there in white as she walked toward me. The smile on her face had been breathtaking and I'd yet to regain mine.

And I couldn't get the words out.

I could feel the panic bubbling up. She was going to think I didn't want to marry her. Oh. Fuck…

Soft fingers cupped my face and I blinked down into those blue eyes that fucking owned me. She smiled softly, lovingly, I could suddenly breathe, could swallow the lump in my throat and

I cleared my throat as I repeated the vows that would bind Marissa and me together for eternity. With the last words, I slipped my ring onto her finger next to her engagement ring and let out a relieved breath.

Then it was her turn, and she swallowed hard a few times before she was able to get the words out as she placed the matching wedding band I'd chosen for us on my finger. A tear spilled down her cheek as she pushed the ring into place and stared down at it as if she were dazed.

I couldn't blame her. This all seemed pretty surreal to me as well. I finally had everything I'd ever wanted, ever dreamed of, standing right in front of me. I'd always been so sure that I'd never been good enough to have this, but here we were, having a man of God pronouncing to the world that we were husband and wife.

There was a roar behind us as everyone stood, clapping and whooping as they called out congratulations and best wishes. I glanced at them for a second before grabbing Marissa's waist and pulling her against me. My gaze went to those luscious lips that were every man's fantasy and my body responded accordingly, instantly hardening and pulsing against her soft stomach as I lowered my head and captured her lips in a kiss that sealed our fate.

I only tasted her for a moment, knowing that now that she was finally my wife I wouldn't be able to control myself as I had been able to do in the past. Now there wasn't anything to keep me from taking what had always been mine. As if she were thinking the same thing, her fingers thrust into my hair to hold me in place for a little longer, her tongue coming out to skim over my bottom lip before she pulled back enough to meet my gaze. "Are you mine, Wroth?"

"Then. Now. Forever," I pledged.

"I think I know what I want for my first tattoo," she surprised me by saying and I threw my head back and laughed in a way that made my soul sing.

"We'll both get it, okay?" I told her and lowered my head to kiss her again.

Everyone was ready to party afterwards but I had other plans. While our friends all got into the vans that had brought us to the warehouse, I bundled Marissa into the back of the limo that had driven her. There wasn't time for a honeymoon but we had two full nights to ourselves before we had to meet up with the tour again. And later, when this fucking tour was over, I would take my girl—my *wife*—on an actual honeymoon wherever she wanted to go.

It took thirty minutes to get to the Hilton and I was thankful for efficient staff as they quickly checked us in. Our bags had already been sent ahead and were waiting for us when I opened the door to our suite and carried Marissa over the threshold. She giggled as I stepped inside and kicked the door shut with my foot before tossing her on the bed.

"Wroth!" she squealed when I bounced on top of her and started to tear the dress from her. "Don't tear my dress."

"Sweetheart, I will buy you twenty of them. Just hush and let me get you naked, okay? I'm dying here, girl." I captured her lips when she started to protest again. I pulled back when I felt the dress rip and gave a satisfied shout as the dress split open down the front. Pushing the material away, I uncovered a sight that would have brought me to my knees if I had been standing.

In white silk panties and matching bra, Marissa looked like a goddess lying beneath me. My entire body began to shake as I attempted to hold my desperate need for her in check. Marissa grinned up at me knowingly, her own body trembling as she lifted her hands and linked her arms around my neck. "I love you, Wroth."

"Love you, too," I got out in a tight rumble as I lowered my head and kissed her.

CHAPTER 27

Marissa

The feel of his hands on my breasts over my bra felt so good. The feel of his hot body through the layers of his uniform was a sweet madness as his dick flexed against my lower stomach. I squirmed against him, seeking a closer connection to that one part of his body that I knew would send me shooting toward the stars.

Calloused fingers tore my bra away just as he had the material of my wedding dress and then those big, rough hands were cupping, pinching, tugging. And I was moaning, crying out his name as my need for him heightened. His lips trailed down my neck and over my chest until he was swallowing one breast almost whole. My back arched off the bed as I sought a deeper connection. "Wroth, please."

"Hush, sweetheart. I'm trying to make this good for you. I don't want to hurt you." He moved from one breast to the other, showing it the same attention he had its twin. "Damn, you taste so good."

While his mouth devoured my pulsing nipple, his hands traveled lower, tearing away my panties as if they were nothing more than tissue paper. I moaned when his fingers found my damp folds and spread the lips of my sex. His thumb rubbed over the little nub that was my clit and then lower, where he rimmed the entrance to my body.

With a growl, he lifted his head. "You're soaking wet, Marissa. I can't wait to be inside of you here." He thrust a finger inside, deep and hard until he was met with the resistance of my virginity. My hips bucked in pleasure, seeking more. Pulling his finger free, he sucked the digit into his mouth, making a groaning rumbly sound in approval at the taste of my need for him.

Before I could beg him for more, he was shifting and replacing his fingers with his mouth and tongue. I gripped the covers underneath me, trying to hold onto my sanity as he licked me from my entrance and upward. When he reached my clit, he sucked it roughly into his mouth, thrusting a finger into my tight channel, and I came apart with his name leaving my lips on a scream of pure unchecked passion.

I wasn't sure how long it took before I realized that I was actually alive and he hadn't in fact killed me with pleasure. When I opened my eyes, he was watching me closely, a dark passion shining at me from those espresso eyes. Wroth had his long, thick dick in his hands as he stroked himself up and down. I'd never seen anything as sexy as the man before me. With a moan, I spread my thighs welcomingly, my need building all over again for him.

"I don't want to hurt you," he assured me in a voice deeper and rougher than any I'd ever heard leave his mouth before. If there had ever been a man who was more beast than human it would have been my delicious husband. "If I do, just say the word and I'll try to stop. Okay?" He was still taking care of me, even now when he looked like he would die if he didn't take me. I didn't think it was possible to love him more than I already did, but in that moment my love grew until it was an ache in my chest.

Licking my lips, I nodded, knowing that even if he did hurt me there was no way I was going to tell him to stop. No way. Carefully, Wroth moved over me, guiding his pulsing dick to my entrance. The tip slid in, stretching me deliciously. I moaned. He'd done that a few times before in the past, and it had always felt so good that I couldn't help but come within minutes. His hips thrust forward just a little and another inch entered me and I moaned his name in approval of how good he felt inside of me.

Wroth rocked back, leaving me completely before entering me again and sinking just a little deeper. Sweat beaded on his brow and rolled down his face as he pulled out again. Moaning, I matched his thrust when he entered me again, the tip of his dick brushing over my hymen. I knew that with the next thrust he would break through it and breathed in deeply when he thrust forward again. There was a sharp pain and I bit the inside of my cheek to keep from crying out. My legs wrapped around his waist to hold him deep inside and I held on tight as my body slowly began to adjust to him.

Wroth lifted his head. "Okay?"

"Better than okay," I assured him as pleasure began to replace the brief pain. I lifted my hips and rubbed against him, grinning in delight when he flexed inside of me. His lids lowered, masking his own desperate need. "Make love to me now, Wroth. You feel so good, honey. I need you so bad."

Wroth growled my name and covered my lips with his as he set a pace that soon had us both touching the stars.

EPILOGUE

Marissa

"Okay, Mrs. Niall. Just a few more minutes and we'll be all set."

I smiled nervously at the nurse as she stood by my head. "Okay," I whispered as I took a few deep breaths to calm my anxiety despite there being tubes sticking in my nose to give me oxygen since I was lying flat on my back.

Wroth rubbed his fingers over my cheek and leaned over to kiss me. "It's okay. You're going to be okay," he kept repeating and I knew he was trying to convince himself more than he was trying to soothe me.

I gave him as bright a smile as I could manage right then, feeling the pressure on my stomach as the three different doctors stood on the other side of the sheet tent. This was it. We were about to be parents. It had only taken three years and two attempts of implanting my harvested eggs mixed with Wroth's impressive swimmers into me through IVF. The first attempt had resulted in none of the embryos taking but the second had been more than successful. So much so that I'd had to be monitored constantly throughout my very rough pregnancy.

When we had first gone through IVF, the doctors had warned that there was a chance that I wouldn't get pregnant just as there was a chance that I could just as easily get pregnant with multiples. Three embryos had taken this time round, and then one had split, producing identical twins. When we'd gone for our first ultrasound and the tech had found four heartbeats, Wroth had nearly fallen out of his seat. He hadn't been the only one startled by the announcement. Our last IVF had been our last shot and I'd known that no matter how many babies we ended up having, they would be our only children. So to discover that we were having four—four little babies—at the same time, I'd been both scared and delighted.

My fear had overridden my delight though when I'd been put on bed rest in my second trimester because the babies were growing at an outrageous rate and too much activity could have easily put me into premature labor. The horror stories of Layla's ordeal with her twins had kept me in bed and scared to so much as sneeze wrong.

Wroth had gone an extra step and hired a nurse to take care of me. Thank God it had been Dallas because I wasn't sure if I would have been able to handle a complete stranger bossing me around like Dallas had done over the last five months. She and Axton, along with their two beautiful kids, had moved into our house on the farm and things had gone pretty smoothly for the most part.

Somehow, by some miracle, I'd actually made it to the thirty-six week milestone without very many more complications and now the doctors thought it was safe to take them. I'd been admitted into the hospital last night and at five thirty this morning the anesthesiologist had come in to prep me for my epidural. Now, we were just minutes away from meeting the rest of our family.

Wroth's hand trembled and I linked our fingers together, offering him the strength he had been giving me since we had decided to start trying for a child of our own. "I love you. Then. Now. Forever," repeating the words that he said to me almost hourly. The same words that we had had inked into our wrists just days after we'd gotten married.

"Then. Now. Forever," he murmured and kissed my lips again.

"You're going to feel a lot of pressure, Marissa." The obstetrician spoke up and I gasped when the pressure he had mentioned left me breathless. It wasn't necessarily painful, but it was scary and a tear leaked from my eyes as I gripped Wroth's hand harder.

"Mari?" Wroth clutched my hand harder and I tried to give him a brave smile as suddenly the pressure was gone and the sound of a screaming baby filled the air. Wroth's head snapped up at the sound of our child crying. When he looked back down at me, he had tears in his espresso eyes. "Mari…"

"We have a boy," the doctor announced and then the pressure started up again as he moved things around inside of me and pulled out another baby. "Say hello to boy number two." Wroth's hold on my hand was nearly to the point that I worried about the bones in my fingers snapping but I just laughed happily as the pressure came again followed by the announcement of yet another son.

The room was full of three screaming little baby boys and they each had their own doctor and nurse working with them as they were checked over and cleaned up. But the doctor wasn't done with me yet and I bit my lip as I waited for the doctors to take the fourth and final baby.

"Okay, here comes baby number four." The doctor called to the last waiting team. "Get ready." The pressure was ten times as bad this time as it had been the first time and I cried out in fear as my screaming child was pulled from my body.

"Well, look what we have here," the doctor said and I froze, scared that something was wrong with my baby.

Wroth stood, even though he'd been told repeatedly to keep on the other side of the tent. When he turned pale I thought it was because something terrible was wrong with our son. One moment he was standing there, his eyes looking almost tortured as he gazed over the tent, and the next he was on the floor, his head bouncing off the chair he'd just been sitting in.

"Wroth!" I screamed just as I heard the doctor give an exasperated sigh. I started to cry. "What's wrong with him? What's wrong with my son?" I demanded. It had to be something bad, why else would Wroth have passed out?

"Nothing," the doctor assured me as a nurse appeared beside my bed and bent to wave something under Wroth's nose. "Except for the lack of a penis, that is. You have a daughter, Marissa. But I'm not so sure that's why your husband passed out. Probably all the gore on this side of the tent." He chuckled and stepped around the tent to show me the screaming, squirming, very angry little girl in his hands. "Say hello to your momma, little princess."

If I hadn't seen the evidence, or rather the lack of evidence, that I really did have a daughter, I wouldn't have believed the doctor. For months now I'd been told repeatedly that I was carrying four boys, two of which were identical. There had been no sign of a girl anywhere. But here she was and as I gazed at her through my tears, I could honestly say that I had never seen a more beautiful baby girl in my life.

From the floor, Wroth groaned and slowly climbed to his feet, holding a bandage to his forehead the nurse had given him. "He's going to need a few stitches," the nurse informed the doctor.

"I'll take care of it myself as soon as I finish with his wife," the doctor assured her, sending Wroth a smirk. "Welcome back, Wroth. Did you notice you have a daughter?"

Wroth's gray face turned ever grayer. "A daughter?" he croaked. His gaze went to our little girl, still screaming at the world angrily and tears fell from his eyes instantly. "She's beautiful." He raked a hand through his hair. "Oh, shit. Shit. I gotta buy a gun."

I turned startled eyes on my husband. His swearing was proof enough that he was upset, but his talk of buying a gun didn't make any sense to me. "What do you mean you have to buy a gun?" I practically screamed. I didn't like guns, and sure as hell didn't want them in our house.

"I have a daughter. I gotta buy a gun, Mari. She's gonna look like you and there will be all kinds of little pricks trying to get into her pants." He stood on shaky legs, only to fall back into his chair. "My head is killing me."

"You probably have a concussion," my doctor informed him calmly. "Sit there and take it easy while we take care of your wife and babies. Then I'll get you stitched up."

"Baby one is perfect," a doctor proclaimed and a nurse appeared by my head with my son wrapped in a blue blanket. "What are we calling this one, momma?"

"Jackson Wroth," I told her, lifting my hand to rub it across the softness of my firstborn's cheek. "Hi there, Jack."

Wroth leaned forward and kissed my lips then the top of our son's head. "Welcome to the outside, son."

Babies two and three were proclaimed perfect as well and were the identical twins. Both were brought over at the same time and I rubbed a finger over their cheeks as well. "Bryant Anthony and Liam James," I gave them each their names, naming them after the men who held such big places in our hearts. We'd decided to hold onto my last name by giving it to one of our sons, and Anthony was Axton's real name. It was only fitting that the man who had become as close to me as my own brother be linked to my child. Liam, who was still doing so well with his sobriety, was a part of our everyday life too. But it had been Wroth who had suggested one of our boys be named after him, adding his own father's name in to complete it.

"Well, this little girl is very angry but healthy," one of the pediatricians announced as he brought over my daughter. He started to hand her over to Wroth, but saw how shaky he still was and leaned her close so that he could kiss her instead. "Do we have a name for this little princess yet?"

I glanced from Wroth to our daughter, not sure what we were going to do. We hadn't had to think about girl's names, and none were coming to mind except for one.

"Can we call her Dorothy?" I asked Wroth.

His eyes widened and he grinned down at me. "Yeah, sweetheart. Dorothy is perfect."

"Dorothy Elizabeth?" I said the name as a question, but it felt right on my tongue and I grinned up at Wroth.

There had been times in my life when I would look at this man and think that this was the happiest day of my life. The first time he told me he loved me. The day we got married. When we found out we were pregnant... But it was now, right at this moment, that I knew I'd never been more happy in my life. And all because of the man sitting right beside me.

"Then. Now. Forever," I whispered.

"I love you, too." He kissed my lips, still holding the bandage to his bleeding head. "Then. Now.   Forever."

ABOUT THE AUTHOR

Terri Anne Browning is a Wall Street Journal and USA TODAY bestselling author. She writes contemporary romance featuring rockers, bikers, and mafiosos-but mostly about the strong female characters who rule what has become known as the Rocker Universe.

Terri Anne lives in Virginia with her husband, their three demons-err, children-and a Frenchie named Ciri.

Follow Terri on Social Media.

TIKTOK
HTTPS://WWW.TIKTOK.COM/@TERRIANNEBROWNING

TWITTER
HTTPS://TWITTER.COM/AUTHORTERRIANNE

AMAZON
HTTPS://AMZN.TO/3AIGPYQ

BOOKBUB
HTTPS://WWW.BOOKBUB.COM/AUTHORS/TERRI-ANNE-BROWNING

FACEBOOK
HTTPS://WWW.FACEBOOK.COM/TERRIANNE.BROWNING

INSTAGRAM
HTTPS://WWW.INSTAGRAM.COM/TERRIANNEBROWNING/

NEWSLETTER
HTTPS://DASHBOARD.MAILERLITE.COM/FORMS/89334/59752074343089173/SHARE

The Rocker Universe Reading Order

OUR BROKEN LOVE COLLECTION
THE ROCKER WHO HOLDS ME
THE ROCKER WHO SAVORS ME
THE ROCKER WHO NEEDS ME
THE ROCKER WHO LOVES ME
THE ROCKER WHO HOLDS HER
THE ROCKERS' BABIES
ANGEL'S HALO JUDGEMENT
ANGEL'S HALO ENTANGLED
ANGEL'S HALO GUARDIAN ANGEL
THE ROCKER WHO WANTS ME
THE ROCKER WHO CHERISHES ME
THE ROCKER WHO SHATTERS ME
THE ROCKER WHO HATES ME
ANGEL'S HALO RECLAIMED
THE ROCKER WHO BETRAYS ME
DEFYING HER MAFIOSO
HIS MAFIOSO PRINCESS
ANGEL'S HALO ATONEMENT
ANGEL'S HALO FALLEN ANGEL
MARRYING HER MAFIOSO
ANGEL'S HALO AVENGED
HER MAFIOSO KING
ANGEL'S HALO FOREVER ANGEL
FOREVER ROCKERS
NEEDING FOREVER VOL 1
CATCHING LUCY
CRAVING LUCY
ROCKING KIN
UN-SHATTERING LUCY
NEEDING THE MEMORIES
TAINTED KISS
TAINTED BUTTERFLY
FOREVER LUCY
TAINTED BASTARD
TAINTED HEARTBREAK

TAINTED FOREVER
NEEDING FOREVER VOL 2
SALVATION
HOLDING MIA
NEEDING NEVAEH
OFF-LIMITS
SWEET AGONY
SAVORING MILA
SURVIVING HIS SCARS
LOVING VIOLET
WANTING SHAW
NEEDING ARELLA
SACRIFICED: SOFIA
SACRED VOW
HER SHELTER
CHERISHING DOE
HEARTLESS SAVAGE
SACRIFICED: CALI
CRUEL SURRENDER
SACRIFICED: ZARIAH
HATING PIPER
SHATTERING TRINITY
HOPELESSLY DEVOTED

ALSO BY, TERRI ANNE BROWNING
(HIS SECRET)
HIS DIRTY LITTLE SECRET
HIS STOLEN SECRET
DEMON'S WINGS COLLECTION